51º

Totally Dead

**Other Streeter Mysteries
by Michael Stone**

The Low End of Nowhere
A Long Reach
Token of Remorse

Totally Dead

A STREETER MYSTERY

Michael Stone

viking

VIKING
Published by the Penguin Group
Penguin Putnam Inc., 375 Hudson Street,
New York, New York 10014, U.S.A.
Penguin Books Ltd, 27 Wrights Lane,
London W8 5TZ, England
Penguin Books Australia Ltd, Ringwood,
Victoria, Australia
Penguin Books Canada Ltd, 10 Alcorn Avenue,
Toronto, Ontario, Canada M4V 3B2
Penguin Books (N.Z.) Ltd, 182–190 Wairau Road,
Auckland 10, New Zealand

Penguin Books Ltd, Registered Offices:
Harmondsworth, Middlesex, England

First published in 1999 by Viking Penguin,
a member of Penguin Putnam Inc.

1   3   5   7   9   10   8   6   4   2

PUBLISHER'S NOTE
This is a work of fiction. Names, characters, places, and incidents either are the product of
the author's imagination or are used fictitiously, and any resemblance to actual persons, living or dead, events, or locales is entirely coincidental.

LIBRARY OF CONGRESS CATALOGING IN PUBLICATION DATA
Stone, Michael, date.
Totally dead : a Streeter mystery / Michael Stone.
p.   cm.
ISBN 0-670-88208-9
I. Title.
PS3569.T64144T68   1999
813'.54—dc21   98-30768

This book is printed on acid-free paper.

Printed in the United States of America
Set in Minion
Designed by Mark Melnick

The author would like to thank and acknowledge Steve and Debbie Anderson, Mary Jane and Bill McBean, Paula Ashen, David Blaska, Phil Reed, Bill Champine, Pat Davidson, Dave Rourke, and Louis Vaccaro.

Totally Dead

1

Patting his tender new hair plugs, the judge glared down at the defendant. Nicholas, Nicky, aka "Space," Lucci: DOB 07/12/76, stared back vacantly from under a scalp shaved slick as Formica. The kid slouched like an amoeba at the table between his lawyer and his investigator. Streeter, the investigator, looked at Lucci and then up at the bench. He recalled how bald the judge had been at the preliminary hearing just a few months earlier. Then he flashed on the Rogaine that he himself had bought recently. Actually, it wasn't Rogaine but, rather, the Walgreen's house brand of minoxidil. Same basic product, same basic purpose.

"Exact identical ingredients but at about half the price of your normal Rogaine," the saleswoman/child had pointed out. "With theirs, you're just paying more for the packaging and advertising. Bells and whistles, like they call it." She nodded with a wisdom beyond her years. Streeter had avoided eye contact with her and instead pretended to be studying the package. When he finally laid out his money, he felt like a sixteen-year-old buying his first box of condoms. He took the stuff home and shoved it, unopened, under his bathroom sink. Since then he'd debated daily with himself whether he really needed the hair restorer. A little middle-aged thinning up there hardly labeled him as balding. Still, why not take the precaution? If Neville Chamberlain had stood up to Hitler back in 1938, he might have avoided the Big War and saved everyone a lot of grief.

Adams County District Judge Steve Griggs shifted his weight on the bench without taking his eyes off young Lucci. His Honor thought of how he'd spent a weekend in bed two months earlier, blurred by pain pills and bourbon that still couldn't take away the intense burning on his scalp. It felt like they'd transplanted a few dozen rows of baby asparagus up there. Paid nearly ten grand for the privilege of suffering like that. The results were decent enough, although no one confused him with Howard Stern. Plus, he knew that half the courthouse had been making Q-ball jokes about him behind his back ever since. Screw them, Griggs thought. He'd recently gotten divorced, and at fifty-seven he had no intention of hitting the cruel dating world looking any older than he had to. If that meant dark plugs and a premium dye job, Judge Griggs was willing to pay the price.

And just look at that stupid little pecker, he now thought as he studied Lucci waiting for the jury to return with its verdict. Eight felony counts stemming from a pair of convenience-store robberies that netted someone a staggering $112 and three small sacks of honey-roasted peanuts. Nicky Lucci had been a serious crystal-meth addict and alcoholic for the better part of five years now. With his head shaved, and his skin pale and blotchy from a fast-food-and-sugar diet, he reminded the judge of an extra from *Schindler's List*. Griggs could almost understand and forgive the drugs and robbery.

That was about pleasure and money. But shaving your head? Utterly senseless. *Why?* the judge thought as he glanced over at the closed door to the jury room. What the hell gets into these kids nowadays? They call that fashion? Goatees and shaved heads. Ass backward, he thought. The hair belongs on top.

Streeter sat up. The sudden motion kicked off a dull ripple of nausea through his stomach and up to his pounding temples. One big-league hangover. He leaned into the defense table, put a hand to his face, and held the bridge of his nose between his thumb and a forefinger. His eyes slid closed as his mouth eased open. A fringe of sweat was forming over his eyebrows. The big investigator tried to remember what-all he'd drunk the night before. But that might be too taxing. All that mattered now was getting through the verdict and going home to rest.

Slowly opening his eyes, Streeter turned to his left and studied Lucci's profile. The guy was all of twenty-one years old and already his life was twisted practically beyond repair. A high-school dropout, a drug addict and alcoholic with a long juvie arrest record and a growing adult rap sheet, no job skills, an IQ most kindly described as resoundingly modest, and an illegitimate daughter he had produced with a teenage nymphomaniac on speed and welfare. Hence his nickname: Space as in Spaced Out. Even in the idiotic crowd of Generation X slackers he hung with, Nicholas Lucci stood out. Shaved head topped with an elaborate red dragon tattoo and black lightning bolts on each temple. Pale-green eyes that registered little besides degrees of confusion and periodic anger, and thin lips surrounded by a goatee the texture of a poorly trimmed paintbrush.

Despite all that, Streeter liked the kid. First of all, he was utterly honest. Of course, with Nicholas, it could be that he was just too lazy to lie. But, still, he was without guile, and

Streeter found that refreshing in his line of work. Most of his criminal clients were surly, mean-spirited, and pathological in avoiding the truth. Second, the kid was genuinely nice. Unwaveringly polite. He always asked how Streeter was doing, how his partner, bail bondsman Frank Dazzler, was, and he usually managed to remember something from their last conversation. Things like "You get those shocks fixed?" or "How's that cavity, Mr. Streeter?" Misguided, clueless, and poly-addicted, true, but Nicky Lucci was not a bad boy at heart. And as with many of his crowd, he aimed most of his destructive behavior squarely at himself.

But most of all Streeter warmed to Lucci because he was innocent of the robberies. In Streeter's practice, that was about as rare as a Nigerian professional ice-hockey player. Now, Nicky wasn't innocent of all charges in all jurisdictions. He was still looking at a fall for auto theft in Boulder County that would certainly keep him in prison into the next millennium. But this armed-robbery stuff in Adams County, just north of Denver, was bogus. Lucci was being framed by one of his "friends," and the more Streeter dug into the case, the more enthused he got. As a bounty hunter with Dazzler Bail Bonds, he also doubled as a private investigator for a few select attorneys, like Don Knight here. Streeter had been in the business about thirteen years, and over that time he'd worked on close to two hundred criminal cases. Nicholas Lucci was maybe his third innocent client. And he wasn't even positive about the other two.

"I don't really know nothing about guns and I was nowhere near those places that got robbed that night," Lucci had told Streeter when he first met him in jail five months earlier. The kid spent a week behind bars before his mother and grandfather made bail. As he looked up at his investigator back then, Nicky's mouth was parted in perpetual bewilderment. He shook his head.

"I was in my room tweaking all night," he'd said, "tweaking" being the street euphemism for mainlining crystal meth. "Why don't they believe me? When they asked about that stolen Porsche up near Louisville, I copped to it on the spot. So why would I bullshit them about those convenience-store holdups?"

Naïve but true. Within a span of a few days, Lucci had been nailed in two separate jurisdictions. Once for suspicion of the store robberies and, in an unrelated matter, for the theft of a new 911. Not only did he admit to stealing the Porsche, he had bragged to everyone he knew about it. But when Streeter interviewed those same people, they all said that Space told them he knew nothing about the robberies. Not to mention that the kid was never known to tote a weapon of any type.

And then there was the state's star witness: Kenny Cobin, with the street name of K-Dog. Kenny had what Streeter discovered to be the ultimate motive for framing Lucci: Kenny was the actual perp. K-Dog was known to pack the same kind of .45 Ruger that was used, and although he was normally penniless, he was seen flashing tens and twenties in the days immediately following the robberies. As Streeter dug into the matter, he found two mutual friends of both Lucci and Cobin who said that K-Dog had all but admitted doing the stores. But Cobin was the first one to the cops, so Lucci got the rap. Luckily, Cobin was a terrible witness on the stand and only one of the convenience-store clerks made even a tentative ID of Lucci from the photo lineup. Attorney Knight had no problem discrediting either in court. It left Streeter wondering why the DA had even bothered going to trial. But prosecutors hate to back off a case—no matter how weak—once they've gone beyond the preliminary hearing.

As they now waited for the verdict, Streeter thought of

how his young client had adamantly refused to let his hair grow out enough at least to cover his cranial tattoos. With his natural red locks, the kid would have come across in court like a befuddled Opie. A better look and decent jury appeal. But no. Space clung to the thuggish street look that made him and his friends as indistinguishable from each other as eggs in a carton. Speaking of looks, the bounty hunter was growing more concerned about his own. Having just turned forty-five, Streeter was noticing the signs of middle age. Thinning hair, fading eyesight, thickening waistline, more pronounced laugh lines, and a hint of jowls. None of it extreme, but to an ex–college football player who always prided himself on his physical condition, it was no fun. Especially now that he had just broken up with yet another girlfriend. Single and not getting any younger. Sitting there, he pondered his hangover. There definitely are good reasons why married men outlive single men, he thought.

Just then, the members of the jury started filing into the courtroom and moving to their seats off to the right of the bench. Knight and Streeter stood up, as did the prosecutor and his investigator at their table. Nicholas Lucci glanced over at the jury box but at first didn't budge. Judge Griggs ordered him to rise. Slowly Nicky obliged. Then Griggs turned to the jury. They'd been out for nearly six hours.

"Madam Foreman, have you reached your verdict?" he asked the intense young Asian woman.

"We have, Your Honor," she responded, glancing at Lucci, who by now had struggled to his feet and stood between his defense team in what might charitably be called a fully upright position.

A good sign, Streeter thought. Juries generally avoid all eye contact with the defendant when they're about to give him bad news. Griggs leaned forward and asked for the verdict. When the first "not guilty" was uttered, Streeter knew they'd get all they were after. If the jury didn't buy Cobin for one count, they wouldn't believe him all the way down the line. Five more times the woman uttered "not guilty." Conspiracy, the whole bit. When she was finished, Streeter glanced to his left. Don Knight was smiling and nodding to no one in particular. Young Lucci was actually yawning while staring at the tabletop in front of him. The bounty hunter leaned over and offered his hand in congratulations.

"Good going, Nicholas," he said. Lucci didn't much like "Nick" or "Nicky" and Streeter refused to honor his street name.

The kid turned slowly toward his investigator and they shook hands. Then he nodded once and said flatly, "I told you I wasn't lying. Why would they come back guilty?"

Streeter didn't know if Lucci was high or really that naïve, so he just nodded back.

From behind them, Nicky's grandparents approached. His grandmother, Maria, reached them first. The boy turned around and looked at her. At all of five feet two in her thick beige heels, Maria Lucci had a round peasant face framed by hair that was surprisingly thick and dark for her seventy-one years. But she had never been pretty, and several wisps of alternately white and black hair now formed a scrawny mustache above her upper lip. Her dark eyes seemed perpetually worried and judgmental. She stared hard at her grandson for a moment and then drew him tightly to a chunky body crowded into a navy-blue dress that covered her from the middle of her throat to her ankles.

"Nicky, my little Nicky," she said into his left shoulder, where her ancient face was buried. The two stood frozen like that for about a minute, until Maria pulled back, her eyes even more concerned. "Our prayers were answered." She nodded solemnly. "But you look terrible, Nicky. We've got to get some food in you." That said, she just kept staring at the boy, one hand clutching each of his bony shoulders.

Nicholas frowned mildly but said nothing. Just then, his grandfather slid between the two, moving Maria's arms down and away with his own small hands. Alphonse Lucci stood only an inch taller than his wife and had the same squat, androgynous body type and pale skin. He squinted up at his grandson through a pair of horn-rimmed glasses with lenses thicker than the windshield on a Brink's truck. Slowly, he shook his head, his thin lips parting in both relief and anger. Then his right hand shot up to the boy's face as Alphonse delivered a flat-handed slap to the cheek.

"What I tell you about those goofwad friends a yours?" the old man asked in a voice deeper and more gravelly than his stature would indicate. "Those little skinhead shits got trouble written all over them." Alphonse nodded quickly for emphasis. He was wearing a black single-breasted suit that looked dated but expensive, a white cotton shirt yellowed slightly from repeated washings, and a plain red tie. "You dodged a bullet on this one, Nicky, but they got that confession for stealing the car. Keep listening to those friends a yours, you'll spend most a your life doing time." He leaned in and craned his head up toward his grandson's face. "You think I'm full of it?"

For his part, Nicholas just stood there perplexed as usual. One hand moved gradually to the cheek his grandfather had struck, but he didn't seem to be in any pain. The old man glanced to his left, to where Streeter and Knight were standing a couple feet away watching. He grabbed Nicholas by his left elbow and moved him out of earshot of the defense team. Maria followed. The three Luccis then drew closer together, the old man talking in hushed tones that Streeter could not make out.

"Now, *he* should talk about friends," Knight said to Streeter. "Did I ever tell you about little Alphonse Lucci?"

Streeter faced the attorney. Don Knight was a few years younger than he was, but with a full head of prematurely white hair and an obvious if low-key cockiness, he seemed older. The bounty hunter shrugged. "Not much. You said he owns a restaurant or something like that and he has sort of a colorful past. I was working on the *kid's* case, so it didn't matter to me what Grandpa was about. As long as he kept paying us, at least."

Knight smiled and glanced back at the Luccis for a second. "Colorful is right. Even if only half of his BS is true, Al Lucci has had some very weird life experiences. He comes from an old West Denver Italian family. They run a few small pizza parlors and they do some catering. Heavy on the Italian food, obviously. That's how he got his nickname: the Cheese Man. The Mexicans in his neighborhood gave it to him and he likes it. Thinks it makes him sound like a hood or something. See, Al has a bad case of Godfatheritis. He likes to think of himself as a power-broker Don-type. Talks about his friends and how he's connected and how he can get things 'done.'" Knight's smile widened. "If you know what I mean. Mostly it's just hot garlic air. If he's even remotely connected to the Mafia, I'm the head of the Aryan Nation. About the only thing old Al can get 'done' is dinner.

"That's not to say his hands are completely clean. He does go in for a little gambling. Sets up card games with his buddies and he's been known to make book on occasion. And from what I hear, he even used to do a little harmless bootlegging. Cigarettes, designer-watch knockoffs, or what have you." The attorney glanced back at the old man. "But he's not nearly what he lets on to be."

Streeter looked over for a second himself. "Frank probably

knows him. Or at least about him." Frank Dazzler was a retired sheriff's deputy and had been a bail bondsman in Denver's Lower Downtown—LoDo—for the past twenty-seven years. He seemed to know personally everyone in town, and he almost certainly knew about anyone who ran a chance of ever needing his services. Nicholas had gotten bail through another bondsman, so the old man's name had never come up before with Frank.

"I'm sure he does," Knight said. "The Cheese Man's been around forever. Mostly downtown and on the West Side. He's one of those guys that, depending on who you ask, you get a whole different version of what he's like. Mostly you'll hear that he's a little loopy and eccentric, but some people will tell you to watch out for him. Me, I like the man. He's rough around the edges, but you know where he's coming from, and he pays up like a good slot machine. Has a daughter, too. The Spaceman's mother. Sheri Lucci. Divorced, and the husband's long-gone. He was a real bad creature, from what Al tells me. The old man says that's where Nicky got his 'moron genes' from. Sheri's sort of a looker, although she's not what you'd call young. Hell, she's probably close to your age, Street."

Streeter shot the lawyer a hard frown. "Ancient, huh?"

Knight smiled and shrugged, holding his palms up innocently. "Come on. Would you want to go to bed with someone that looked your age?"

Streeter ignored the crack. "Why isn't she here?"

Knight shrugged again. "She had some sort of business up in Vail this morning and she was going to try and make it back by now. Who knows what happened?"

Just then, the Lucci family meeting broke up. Maria and Nicholas headed toward the rear courtroom exit without even a look back. Alphonse watched them leave and then approached the lawyer and investigator.

"Mr. Streeter, I'm Alphonse Lucci," the little man said firmly as he extended his hand. "You can call me Al. Don here tells me you did a hell of a job for Nicky."

Streeter shook the hand and watched as Al nodded repeatedly in stern concentration, his head bobbing loosely over a collar that was too big for his neck. His suit seemed at least one size too large, and it made the little man look vulnerable. Not weak, but gentle.

"Thank you, Al. It was obvious that the boy didn't rob those stores."

"No, *thank you*, Mr. Streeter. See, nothing's obvious with Nicky, and if you can make any sense at all outa those eight balls he runs around with, you're a wizard of a detective. World-class." He studied Streeter for a moment. "If there's ever anything I can do for you, just let me know. Anything at all. Alphonse Lucci never forgets stuff like this, and I know a lot of people around town. I know everyone worth knowing. You keep that in mind."

It sounded like half a boast, half a threat. "I'll do that."

Al seemed pleased with the response and he smiled, his head still wobbling in a nod. "Good boy," he concluded, lifting his open hand up near Streeter's face as if he was about to give him a friendly slap on the cheek. Then he pulled the hand down. "Good boy," he repeated. "I never forget." With that, he turned and headed toward the back of the room.

2

The night he burned down the wrong house, Mitch Bosco was in a rare mood: stone sober, focused, and confident. So much for rare moods. Before he got out of his car, parked a few hundred yards from the place, he had even rechecked the address in the dirty glow of his flashlight. There it was, 446 Mountain Way, West Vail. The guy who hired him had described the place as a large wood-and-glass custom home near the beginning of a two-block cul-de-sac, just north of the mountainside. Sure, he had warned Mitch that Mountain Way twisted off at an odd angle and it would be hard to determine exact compass directions. Especially at two in the morning. But with the address in hand, Mitch was sure that he'd get it right. As the self-help tape he'd listened to on the way up had warned him, preparation and concentration are the cornerstones to achievement.

So much for confidence. If you wrote down 446 Mountain Way and the man actually told you to torch 448, you've got a problem no matter how intent you are or how clear-headed you might be at that particular moment.

Not that arson really was Mitch's specialty. Arson, drug running, extortion, burglary, armed robbery, and the occasional Ponzi scheme—he did them all with about the same level of slightly better-than-average competence. Diversity of skills ensures your marketability. Mitch had read something to that effect two years earlier when he first embarked on his "Ladder of Success." That's what he'd labeled his self-improvement jag in his "Prosperity Journal" back then. And he was dead serious about the whole thing. Back on his fortieth birthday, Mitch Bosco had done some serious soul-searching and had decided to turn his life around. He knew he would never be a real citizen with an actual job and benefits, paying withholding taxes and all. That, obviously, was not Mitch. But if he was going to be an outlaw, he determined to be the best outlaw he could be and to make it profitable. So he immersed himself in the works of all the self-help gurus. Anthony Robbins, Stephen Covey, M. Scott Peck, and the like. Even dabbled in New Age spirituality. He'd read scores of books, attended dozens of workshops, and listened to countless hours of tapes. And he chronicled it all in the "Prosperity Journal" he carried with him always.

Actually, except for its being the wrong house, Mitch did an outstanding job that morning. He lugged eight large bags of cheap, greasy potato chips to the house, broke in effortlessly through a rear kitchen door, and then scattered the chips thickly throughout the living-room and dining-room floor as well as on most of the overstuffed furniture. A firefighter he knew in Denver had told him once that greasy potato chips make the perfect accelerant for an arson. They burn quick and hot, and they're all but impossible to trace. Mitch lit the chips in about four different spots with the large farmer matches he'd brought and then he put the burned matches in his pocket. He'd long ago learned that no detail is too insignificant if you want to be the best.

The first floor was going like a dry Christmas tree before he even got back outside. In fact, the whole place was starting to burn real good a couple of minutes later, as Mitch stood off to the side for a bit, admiring his master-piece. Feeling the warm glow of the flames washing over his face in the early-October mountain air, he felt proud and competent. The place was vacant, as the man had said it would be. Most of the houses up there were during the week at that time of year: too early for skiing and too cool for summer sports. Mitch wished he'd brought a camera to record his creation. Later, jogging back to the car, he couldn't wait to return to Denver to tell the man how well the job went. With the kind of guy Mitch was working for, Freddy Disanto, the only news you wanted to deliver was good news.

Once he got to his Volvo station wagon and started moving toward the highway, Mitch lit a Salem 100 and smiled. He knew he'd be on I-70, past Vail and probably beyond East Vail, by the time the tiny rural fire department made it to the scene. Even if the firefighters got there quickly, which they seldom did, in these remote places they never had anything like enough water to do much good. Their job really was just to make sure that everyone got out safely and that none of the neighboring houses went up. As he moved the Volvo onto the highway entrance ramp, Mitch grabbed the pint of ginger schnapps from the seat next to him and took a quick pull. Sure, he knew that "absolute self-control" was rule eight on his *Complete Success* tape and that smoking and drinking definitely didn't fit into that category. He knew he'd have to work on those two. Maybe even write about them in his journal. Still, being confident was one thing, but as Mitch Bosco rolled onto the freeway he knew that "absolute self-control" in the form of sobriety was not in his near future. He was only human, he reminded himself.

Sheri Lucci took three quick puffs from her Virginia Slim and then snuffed it into an ashtray on the kitchen counter. She had been *seriously* trying to quit smoking for about six months now, and she was down to the point where she'd allow herself seven cigarettes a day. Maybe eight. Even then, she'd go no farther than halfway into the thing before putting it out. Seven cigarettes a day except for times like now. Nights when she'd wake up after a couple fitful hours of sleep and lie in bed knowing it would be a good long time before she'd nod off again. All bets were off when that happened. She'd get up, put on her robe, pace the house, and have a few cigarettes until she got drowsy. And those nights were coming more often lately.

Usually, Sheri could put her finger on what caused the insomnia: Her wacky family, money troubles, not having a man. Or having the wrong one. Tonight, it was her son. Nicky getting his verdict that afternoon and her being stuck up in Vail trying to set up a catering operation for her father. Alphonse was convinced that he should expand his business outside of Denver. More money. Not to mention that the old man was getting pressure to close up his pizza parlors in town. The Vail Valley, with its constant weddings, business meetings, and parties, was the place he chose to go first. Sheri had been trying to connect with local sources and feel out the help situation for the past month. But this was the first time the work went so late into the evening. Spending the night at the Lucci vacation home on Mountain Way made more sense than driving two hours back to Denver. Especially seeing as how she'd missed Nicky's verdict by several hours anyhow. Sheri had worked for Alphonse ever since that useless boner she'd married and had a child with left her sixteen years ago. She adored her father. What the Cheese Man wanted, she did her best to provide.

At least Nicky beat that robbery nonsense, Sheri thought as she lit another Slim and pushed back at the long brown hair flowing into her eyes. Poor lost Nicky. She couldn't specifically remember dropping him on his head while he was still in diapers, but she and her husband were so deep into coke and pot back then that she figured something like that must have happened. How else could you explain her son? Dull-witted and utterly lacking direction, her Nicholas was a chip off the old blockhead. Just like his father, Donny Scarpetto. But, sadly, without his looks, muscles, and street-lacquered charisma. Poor lost Nicky, she thought again as she moved silently around the huge kitchen, illuminated only by a small lamp in the next room. No prison time for the armed robbery. A silly charge from the word "go." As if Nicky could find a gun and the *cojones* to use it in a stunt like that. But he'd surely be going away for that numbskull car theft up near Boulder, and that troubled his mother, getting her up just before 2 A.M. to pace the kitchen.

Studying her reflection in the darkened microwave door, Sheri put out the cigarette. Her eyes didn't look too tired and she took pride in her wrinkle-free face. Not bad for forty-two. If she could keep her weight in check, which she usually did, Sheri Lucci could still turn a head or two. At least her legs and butt were holding up, she thought. God, it was sad watching some women her age or even younger at the gym. No matter how many hours they spent in the aerobics room, their rear ends sagged like old pillows over legs growing chunkier by the month.

Sheri coughed once and figured she'd take another whack at sleep. But before she could empty the ashtray, she noticed a flicker of light coming from outside the kitchen window—from next door, the place owned by that arrogant gynecologist from Mexico City. Sheri had only met the man, Omar something-or-other, once, when he'd come up to ski a couple of years earlier. The jerk practically stared right through her clothes on their first meeting. With Alphonse and Maria standing next to her out on the back deck and Omar's wife all of three feet away, for crying out loud.

Sheri put down the ashtray and moved to the west window, leaning over the sill and straining her eyes. The first floor on that side was going up in flames as she watched. Luckily, the houses up there were spaced close to a hundred feet apart. Flames were shooting out every window and spreading to the second floor. Within a couple of minutes, as Sheri watched in horror, the entire building seemed to be engulfed. She shook her head to clear it and then grabbed the phone to call 911. No way they'd save Omar the hard-on's place, but at least she could protect the Lucci house. Then, as she gave the groggy dispatcher the necessary information, Sheri saw him. His profile standing about thirty feet from her back deck, facing the burning building. In the flickering light, she could see that the man was about average height, a little overweight, and bald except for the thick fringe of dark hair around the temples and back. Seemed to have a dense mustache, too, and long narrow sideburns. As he turned briefly in her direction, he seemed to be smiling. The guy stood there for a moment more and then turned away from Omar's, breaking into a slow trot out around behind her house and heading east.

After she'd hung up, Sheri lit another cigarette and thought how familiar the man looked. It was the longish hair on the sides and back of the shiny scalp. She hated it when bald men tried to make up for it by growing what little hair they had longish like that. Then it came to her. She crushed the cigarette and picked up the phone again. Alphonse answered on the fifth ring.

"What the hell?" he asked, his voice dry from sleeping with his mouth open.

"It's me. Sheri."

"Sheri?" He said the word quickly and waited.

"Yes."

"This better be important, honey." His voice rose but stayed hoarse.

"The place next door up here. The one owned by that horny Mexican doctor. It's on fire. It'll be history in about five minutes. Unfortunately, the doctor isn't inside."

Nothing at first, and then he spoke irritably. "If I was a horny Mexican doctor, that might sound important. But I'm not." No one spoke for a moment, so he added, "Is our place in any danger?"

"I doubt it." Sheri was getting a little angry herself. "I called the fire department and they should get here in time to save us. They'll probably just watch it for a while and then a couple of them'll hit on me. Like that time we had the propane leak."

"Are you all right?"

"Yes. And thanks for asking." After a beat. "Finally."

"Look, honey, I could tell by your voice you weren't in any real trouble."

She knew that, too. From before the time she could walk, her father had instilled a sense of old-country toughness in her. He really wanted a son, but, since he didn't get one, there was no way on earth he was about to settle for a *weak* daughter. And the lesson was not wasted on Sheri. Generally—that is, except when it came to men. "Listen, Daddy, it was an arson and I saw the guy who did it."

"You're kidding." The Cheese Man was sitting up now

and had put his glasses on. "That horny doctor must have some real enemies. Either that or he's got financial troubles and he's using a little Jewish lightning to bail himself out. The place was probably insured to the hilt."

"I don't think that it's his enemies you should be worried about. The guy who did it, I'm pretty sure he's one of those clowns working for your friend Disanto. That bald moron with the funny eyes. Almost looks like they're crossed. I don't remember his name."

Al stared at the opposite wall for a long time without answering. Finally, "I know who you mean. But why would they burn down the doctor's house?"

Sheri shrugged and reached for another Virginia Slim. The light from the flames was so bright by now that she took a step back from the window. In the distance she could hear the fire-engine sirens wailing. "Those guys, who knows? But with all the bad blood between you and Freddy the D., it's a pretty safe bet that our neighbor had nothing to do with this."

"No doubt about that, honey. That damned Disanto'll stop at nothing to get me out." Al nodded to the opposite wall. "Maybe it's a warning. Maybe they think I'll figure I'm next and have a heart attack or something."

Both of them were silent for a long time. Sheri finally crushed her cigarette and spoke. "You want me to tell the cops about this?"

The old man shook his head wildly. "No. As far as they know, all you saw was the fire. Luccis take care of their own problems." He paused. "Their own way. Besides, with Disanto, you send the cops after him and it'll only make him more pissed. And more determined to get to me."

"I thought you'd say that." She paused for a moment. "Look, Daddy, I think you should consider the man's offer. Arson is pretty serious business."

Al said nothing for a long time. "Maybe you're right. Maybe, but I doubt it. Just try to get some sleep for now and then head back down here first thing in the morning. I think I know who to go to with this. Someone to help out."

"Who's that?"

"No one you know, honey. Just you try to get some sleep." He hung up without either of them saying good night. As he sat there in the dark, Alphonse took off his heavy glasses and returned them to the nightstand. He thought about the big private eye who'd kept his grandson out of jail. If this Streeter could make a clod like Nicky look good, he could probably deal with a slimeball like Freddy Disanto. He recalled the shoulders on Streeter. Wide as a doorframe. At least maybe he could throw a scare into Disanto. Get the guy to back off some. The Cheese Man made a mental note to call Don Knight in the morning and get Streeter's number. Then he farted dully into his flannel pajamas and crawled back under the covers.

3

When Streeter first moved to LoDo in the mid-eighties, it felt like he was living in an Edward Hopper painting. But by now it had become little more than a gathering place for Yuppies and tourists. Overpriced, with parking that required time, money, and patience. Plenty of all three. Streeter lived on its fringes and he liked LoDo less all the time. As recently as six years ago, he'd been surrounded by sad, ancient warehouses, dangerous bars, and the funky old Union Station. Then along came Coors Stadium and the Colorado Rockies. Streeter seldom went there. It reminded him of a boutique shopping mall/food court that happened to have a ball field in the middle. In the early seventies, when he had played football at Western Michigan University, he and his friends used to go to baseball games in Chicago, Detroit, and Milwaukee: Wrigley Field, the old Comiskey Park, Tiger Stadium, and County Stadium. Those were real ballparks—rickety old structures where large Polish and

German Americans smoked cigarettes openly, ate and drank too much, and settled their differences on the spot, usually with their fists.

Not that Streeter liked urban decay and violence. It's just that he thought Coors Stadium and the surrounding bar scene was overdone, oversanitized, and oversaturated. He kept waiting for some of the watering holes to belly up. There must be fifty of the joints by now, with more planned. The whole place just tried too hard. Even though Streeter lived within about ten blocks of the heart of LoDo, he no longer felt any real connection to it.

Parking now in front of the renovated church where he and Frank worked and lived, Streeter still ached from his hangover. Never one for napping, he figured he'd catch a good workout in his basement weight room. If he *had* to show signs of age on his hairline, he figured he could at least keep his body toned. Streeter had worked out daily for years, to the point where his six-foot-two-inch frame was wrapped with almost two hundred twenty pounds of firm muscles. Following his workout, he'd take a hot shower, maybe have dinner with Frank, and go to bed early. No Johnnie Walker Red tonight, he thought as he headed to the front door. Well, certainly no more than a nightcap.

Streeter loved the church. Frank Dazzler had bought the place some twenty-five years earlier for a tiny fraction of what it was now worth. He fixed the building up and rented out space on the first floor to a women's gym and self-defense school. His office and apartment took up the rest of that floor, and Streeter lived upstairs, in a spacious loft apartment that had been his home for more than twelve years. It housed his vast book collection as well as his baby-grand piano. He'd gotten the thing a couple of years earlier, as collateral on a bond, and he'd been struggling to master it ever since. His books, his loft, his piano, his weights. Having his stuff around him seemed more important the older he got.

Even though his life wasn't feeling like a picnic these days, he did have his place and he did have Frank Dazzler, who meant more to him than his own family, dysfunctional and long-gone as they were. He and Frank had first met years ago, when the bondsman came to the country-and-western bar where Streeter was working as a part-time bouncer. With his size and strength, and the controlled demeanor of a veteran cop, he was a sought-after doorman. He also worked days as an accountant, his haphazard career path the result of dropping out of college halfway through and then letting circumstances make his choices for him over the next ten years. At any rate, Frank was looking for a bail jumper that night and his search took him to the joint Streeter was working. He instantly saw potential in the big, thoughtful man. Within days, Streeter was working for Frank, and he moved into the loft shortly after that.

Now, opening the huge wooden front door directly beneath a broken neon JESUS SAVES sign, Streeter turned around to see his partner walking toward him on the sidewalk. A few years earlier, in his mid-sixties, Frank had suddenly converted to exercise. He created his own form of race-walking/jogging that he stuck to religiously.

"Hey, Street." Frank lifted one hand in a wave as he got close. His face perked up. "How'd your verdict go down today?"

Streeter held the door open. "Not guilty on all counts. You know how often that happens?"

"As a general rule, approximately never," Frank said as he reached the door. He was wearing baggy gray sweatpants, black-and-white running shoes, and a sweatshirt that at one point had undoubtedly been white. "Congratulations. I know you worked like a maniac for that kid." Frank studied him. "What's wrong? You don't seem too happy about it. Come to think of it, you don't look too hot, either. Sort of like Keith Richards on a bad hair day."

The bounty hunter cleared his throat. "I'm a little under the weather from last night. I went out for a few hoists with some of the boys and I must have overdone it."

Frank frowned. "A case of the old whips and jangles today, huh?" The frown deepened. "You know, you've been overdoing it pretty often lately." He walked into the church foyer, with Streeter following. They went down the hallway to the right, toward Frank's office. "Must be something bugging you if you're drinking like that," he mentioned when they got there.

Streeter didn't respond. Frank walked behind his large wooden desk and flopped down on his overstuffed swivel chair. His partner moved toward the desk and leaned against the back of the chair, his hands resting on the top of it. He remained silent.

"Don't know, huh?" Frank bent over and untied his running shoes, letting out a hiccup of a grunt as he did. When he straightened back up, he could see that Streeter had sat down. "My hunch is it has something to do with that Connie Nolan lady. The guitar teacher. You two been broken up for a couple of months now, and I thought that was pretty much behind you. But who knows? Maybe it's bothering you more than you realize."

Streeter looked off to the side. Connie taught at the music school where he used to take piano lessons. He'd met her while working a tough PI case six months earlier. They had started dating, and everything was going well until he discovered she was still sleeping with an old boyfriend. An ex-fiancé, actually, who turned out to be more of a fiancé than an ex. The discovery came two weeks after Streeter and she had agreed to have an exclusive relationship. Now, as he turned back to Frank, he shook his head.

"It's probably not really Connie, Frank. More like a hundred Connies. She was just another one that didn't work out." He shrugged and let out a quick grin. "I don't know. Sometimes I wonder if it's worth it. I mean this whole woman thing."

"Oh, I think we both know it's almost always worth it." Frank leaned into his desk and looked closely at the other man.

"Maybe, maybe not," Streeter said. "But for whatever reason, I haven't been sleeping all that well lately." He adjusted himself in his seat. "You know, Frank, it's not like I'm getting any younger, either. My pants seem to be shrinking in the vicinity of my waist, my hair's starting to show some serious lack of interest in staying on my head, and there's times I'd like to iron my face. All my living and promise seems to be in the past. I feel like I've got a great future *behind* me."

Frank broke into a broad grin and sat back. "Yeah, there's always that aging deal. Tell the truth, I was thinking about getting you a walker for Christmas." He shook his head but kept smiling. "Come on, Street. You're—what—forty-five and change. From where I'm sitting, you got the best years of your life ahead of you." Then he leaned in again. "But if I was you, I'd give it a rest with the ladies for a while. That's never been your strong suit. Four failed marriages and how many engagements that misfired? Then that revolving door with all the rest of them, who usually were the type to give 'high-maintenance' a new meaning. I never did understand your selection process. Put your mind on something else for a while." He winked. "And lighten up. Hitting the bottle isn't going to take care of business for you. It's not like you don't have a life on your own."

Streeter considered that and nodded. "You're probably right about that."

"Damned straight I'm right, partner. Take a look at most of those bozos you work with. Like that Lucci kid. I see the mess guys like him make out of their lives and, from where I'm sitting, you and me are doing pretty good. Just count your blessings and chill out. That famous intensity of yours might help when you're out on a job, but it must be a royal pain in the ass in your social life."

"It can be." He studied Frank and said nothing for a moment. "Keep putting me on the right track, okay? I hate being a whiner, and that's just how I've been feeling this past couple of months."

"I noticed." Frank nodded. "It's time to move on. You need a good hot case to shift your mind off of you and on to something else. This woman thing, it'll work itself out when you're ready for it. Listen, I'm gonna go take a shower. Got a date tonight with you-know-who." He stood up, nodded again, and left the room.

Streeter sank back in his chair. Frank had been dating the owner of the women's gym in the church for the past several years. Although the topic of marriage never came up between them, they had a solid bond that they both enjoyed. They were good together, and that thought made Streeter smile. He stood and went up to his loft. When he got there, he stared at the cherrywood piano and decided to tackle a little more Chopin before hitting the weights. His hangover was just about gone. Talking to Frank usually left him in a better mood. He went to his refrigerator and grabbed a bottle of water and then sat down at the keyboard. Glancing at the piano, he noticed a stack of mail he'd been ignoring. Being involved in a trial usually threw his normal routine off, and there was at least a week's worth. He started leafing through the stack but stopped when he saw a postcard featuring a panoramic view of the Chicago Loop, on the shores of Lake Michigan. Turning the card over, he saw cramped but neat writing on the back. He set the rest of the stack down next to him on the bench and read the card.

"Streeter—It's a voice from your past. Ronnie Taggert. I hope you haven't forgotten me. I'll be back in Denver by Friday the 16th. I'd like to get together with you and discuss a business proposition. I'll call you then. Yours, Ronnie. P.S. I hope you lost that miserable Moffatt broad by now."

His mouth creased in a confused half-smile. Ronnie Taggert had been involved in a case he had worked on three years earlier. At the time, she was a paralegal for the most corrupt lawyer Streeter had ever met. The lawyer didn't survive the proceedings, but Ronnie did, even if it meant she had to leave the state. Ronnie Taggert always was a survivor, regardless of what she had to do. And talk about a sexy profile. Not to mention an attitude. Ronnie was smolderingly attractive, but in a casual way that most women could never approach, no matter how hard they tried. Ronnie had turned out to be good people, helping Streeter sort out one very weird mess of a case, although she gave off a definite troubled and distant vibe.

He also flashed on "that miserable Moffatt broad" and frowned. Story Moffatt was one of the main characters in the case. When it was over, she and Streeter had a brief fling, but he hadn't seen her in over two years now. Which was fine with him.

"Business proposition?" he asked softly, out loud to the empty room. His eyebrows shot up and he tossed the card back on top of the piano. He realized that the 16th was the day after tomorrow. Then he turned his attention back to Chopin.

4

Alphonse Lucci's office was decorated in a style that the original Frank Sinatra–Dean Martin Rat Pack would have loved. At least Alphonse liked to think so. Located behind his catering kitchens, it had a single small window covered by towel-thick burgundy drapes. The furniture was low, dark Mediterranean with lamps heavy enough to stop a moving mid-sized car. The shag carpeting was the color of dried blood, and the paneled walls boasted autographed photos of aging or dead crooners like Bobby Darin and Vic Damone.

"So what makes you think this guy can help us?" Sheri Lucci asked as she adjusted herself in a chair in front of her father's desk, toying with the Virginia Slim. She hadn't gotten back to sleep after the fire that morning, and she was in no mood to waste time.

"I told you. He did a bang-up job on Nicky's case." Alphonse was sitting up ramrod straight at his desk. "Not to mention, he's big enough to put a little fear into that schmuck Disanto and yet he won't lose his cool and get carried away. At least that's according to Knight, anyhow. We had us a long talk this morning about Mr. Streeter. Knight says he's the best skip tracer around and he's relentless when he takes on a project." The old man nodded. "Besides, who else am I gonna send over there to talk to Disanto. Maria? Nicky? One of my delivery guys?" He paused. "You?" He waved his hand in disgust and turned away for a moment. "Arson is pretty serious stuff. What if they'd torched our place instead of the Mexican's and you were asleep?"

Sheri put the cigarette back into the pack. Slowly she smoothed out the front of her red skirt. "So you're hiring this musclehead to toss Freddy around?"

The Cheese Man shook his head impatiently. "No, no, no. Just to have him go visit the dipshit and reason with him. I called Streeter before and he said he'd be here at three. Stick around. It's just a few minutes until then. Who knows? Maybe he'll have some ideas a his own."

"What does he look like?" Sheri sat up slightly.

Her father frowned. "The back end of a mule. What do you care? Let's put our libido on hold for a while here, honey. Think you can handle that? I swear, if you'd a married a decent man instead a that oversexed greaseball you hooked up with way back when, maybe all our lives would be a lot better off." Then his voice softened in concern. "You wouldn't have to act like you're on the make all the time, and maybe Nicky wouldn't a turned out so screwed up, either."

Sheri's eyes narrowed. "Can we not go through all that again, Daddy? Please."

Alphonse's eyebrows shot up, he shrugged, and then sat back in his chair while pulling once on his red tie. He was wearing the same basic outfit he'd had on at the trial.

Alphonse Lucci had about a dozen of the dark suits and an equal number of white shirts and red ties. Other than his pajamas, that was about all he ever seemed to wear.

"Okay, okay," he said. "But listen, when Streeter gets here, tell him you're not exactly sure who torched the place this morning—you just have a good idea. From what Knight tells me, Streeter'll insist on us going to the cops with that. I don't want them nosing around if I can handle it on my own. They'll be all over us and it'll end up with them leaning on me for my card games. Just tell Streeter it might a been Bosco and that we're covering our asses in case Disanto sent him."

Sheri nodded. They sat there in silence for a moment, the room smelling like baking dough and onions. She was about to say something when there was a knock on the door. Both Luccis turned in that direction; Alphonse spoke first. "It's not locked. Come on in."

Streeter recognized the Cheese Man's voice through the door. He pushed it open and walked into the stuffy office. Somehow, he wasn't surprised at the decor. Or the lighting, which was along the lines of Marlon Brando's office in the opening wedding scenes of *Godfather I*. Alphonse stood up behind the large desk. At least, Streeter thought the little man was standing. In a low chair across the desk sat a woman he estimated to be about forty, fit-looking in a tight red skirt and a white cotton blouse. She had brown eyes nearly as dark as Al's and brown hair. It was styled in a longish sixties bob cut with short bangs in front. When she saw him, she broke into a friendly smile. Streeter nodded at her and then looked back at Alphonse.

"Mr. Lucci." He walked toward the desk.

"Hey, come on." Alphonse took two quick steps to the side of his desk. "What I tell you yesterday? It's Al." He paused and frowned into his dense glasses. "Is there anything I can call you besides 'Mr. Streeter'? I'd like to keep this informal here. All in the family." He nodded toward Sheri.

Streeter glanced down at the woman, who was turned in his direction. Then he looked back at Al. "Just plain Streeter's fine."

The old man considered that, his smile dropping. "Done." Then he pointed at Sheri. "This is my daughter, Sheri Lucci. Nicky's mother."

Sheri nodded and extended her hand to be shaken, still smiling. "I've heard a lot of good things about you, Streeter. From Daddy and from Nicky." She paused as they shook hands. "I'm sorry I didn't make it to court yesterday, but I was up in Vail, swamped with business. Thanks so much for helping my son."

Streeter nodded. Al pointed to a chair next to his daughter, and the bounty hunter sat down. Sheri studied Streeter. He was wearing an expensive-looking white Oxford shirt, the kind with those band collars that she liked. Even in the long sleeves she could see that his arms were thick and his chest strained slightly against the fabric as well. Her father was right. A guy with shoulders like this would give Freddy Disanto something to think about. Finally, she broke the silence. "Nicky's no angel, but he would never go out with a gun and rob someone."

"That was pretty clear from early on," Streeter said. "But he's not out of the woods yet. No offense, Sheri, but your son's pretty troubled. Underneath it all he's a good kid, but he's dug a real hole for himself in a lot of ways."

Sheri liked the way he leaned toward her as he spoke. A low, confidential voice and intense eyes. He seemed sincere, but not preachy.

Alphonse sat down and cleared his throat. It sounded like he had a cold. "Well, Nicky's not why I wanted to talk to

you, Streeter." His voice was deeper now and it had a definite no-nonsense tone that caused both of them to look at
him. "First off, can I have Sheri here get you anything?
Coffee? Pop?"

"No thanks."

The Cheese Man nodded and picked up the water glass in
front of him. He took a short sip, set it back down, and then
ran through the whole story about the Vail arson. "Arson,"
he repeated softly when he'd finished. His voice picked up
again as he stared at Streeter. "If Sheri here's right about
who she saw up there, then my hunch is that a Mr. Freddy
Disanto was behind it." He sat back, his head looking a
shade too big for his shoulders.

"You think this guy had your neighbor's house torched to
get at you?" Streeter frowned and turned to Sheri. "How
sure are you about seeing Mitch Bosco?"

"I only saw him for a couple of seconds. I couldn't even
describe him very well to the police, but I think it was him."

The bounty hunter looked back at the man behind the
desk. After Al had called him that morning, he'd asked
Frank if he knew anything about the Cheese Man. The
bondsman echoed what Don Knight had said: that Alphonse
was sort of a marginal criminal in years past, but now he was
just a harmless old man who ran a few card games that
weren't entirely legal. "Does Bosco work for Disanto?"

"Not all the time. Mitch is sort of a freelancer, from what
I hear. You need something like this done, you call him. But
the D. has used him in the past, the way I hear it. Freddy
likes to dabble in different vices and he's had uses for a guy
like Mitch over the years. See, Freddy can be a rough customer. I heard he even killed a guy once, but that's just
rumors."

Streeter nodded. "Why did they do it, Al? I mean, why
your neighbor's house?"

"I'll put all my cards on the table here, Streeter." He glanced at Sheri, and then looked back at Streeter and leaned forward, his voice taking on a hushed, intense tone. "I'm sure I've made a few enemies over the years, but of all of them Freddy the D. is the biggest asshole. He's let certain mutual friends know that he hates my guts and that he'd like to see me suffer more than a little. As to why he'd go after the doctor's house is anybody's guess, but my hunch is that he meant it as a warning to me. That, or maybe they just screwed up and got the wrong place. Who knows? But my hunch is that he did it as a negotiating tactic." Alphonse's eyes flared open wide and he nodded sagely, as though that should explain everything.

"What does that mean?" Streeter shifted in his seat.

"The D. wants to buy Daddy out but he's not selling," Sheri interjected.

"You see, Streeter," Al stepped in now, "Freddy owns a few restaurants down south, near Englewood, and he wants to expand up here on the near West Side. He's becoming a regular developer, too. One a my two pizza joints is in a choice area where Freddy wants to locate, so he tried to buy me out. It's the one over off 32nd Street he's really hot for. Now, I've got about as much interest in retiring as Tiger Woods has, so I told the D. absolutely no. He didn't much care for the answer, and lately he's been making rumblings about 'convincing' me I'm making a big mistake. I run a card game Monday nights, and the D. sits in usually. He's been giving me grief about it for the last couple a months. Since I turned down his offer."

Streeter leaned back. "You're telling me he'd order an arson fire because you won't sell him one of your restaurants. You must serve some terrific lasagna there, Al."

"Pizza mostly," the old man said with obvious pride. "Opened that one right after the Big War with my old man, may he rest in peace. Nineteen hundred and forty-six. It's an institution up here. But there's something else for Disanto. He's already bought up every house and business on the block over there off 32nd and him and some friends plan on making a condo and shopping complex out of the neighborhood. My place would be sort of a anchor restaurant for the project, it being so established and all. That's not sitting well with the D. You know, one stubborn old hump like me in his way. And I understand some of his partners are getting pretty impatient, what with Freddy promising they'd own the whole block by now. There's a lot a money riding on it, and his people are leaning on him to get the job done."

Streeter shook his head. "But arson. This is like the movies." He paused. "Did he make you a good offer?"

"Sure did," Sheri shot in.

"No amount a money gets me to sell that place," Alphonse said intensely. "It's in the family as long as I'm alive. It was a promise I made to my old man. The D. knows that." He looked off for a moment. "Freddy's got a personal reason, too."

"What's that?"

Alphonse looked off again before answering. "I don't want to go into too much detail, but I did some business with Disanto's old man a while back. Must be ten, twelve years ago. All you have to know is that it involved a shipment of bootleg videos from California and it went sour. Real sour. Ended up with Disanto's father, Carlo, and his brother, I forget the name, both going to jail. Anyhow, this bastard Freddy blames me for the whole screwup, and he's pissed because his father died of emphysema down in Canon City a year or so after he went away. Freddy thinks I'm responsible for Carlo dying." Alphonse shrugged dramatically. "Like I made the guy smoke three packs a day for forty-plus years. Gimme a break."

"Have you told the police about this?" the bounty hunter asked.

Alphonse shook his head violently. "No way. It's all just speculation for now, and besides, you think I want to sit down with a bunch of police detectives and explain a bootleg-video scam? Or my card games? I don't need them digging into my business. Past or present."

Streeter studied the man across from him. His head so wrinkled, and him squinting behind those thick glasses. He leaned toward the desk. "That leaves us with the big question: what does all this have to do with me?"

"Right to the point, huh?" Alphonse asked, smiling now. "I like that." He leaned forward even farther. "Here's the deal, Streeter. I want to go rattle this Disanto's cage a little. Let him know that, if he did this fire and he's thinking about pulling any more bullshit like that, well, sir, it'll cost him. Come outa his hide." Alphonse was getting excited as he spoke, and a thin line of spit came out of the side of his mouth. He wiped awkwardly at it, missing by inches. "Big guy like you oughta handle that easy. Let Disanto know we got suspicions here and that Alphonse Lucci ain't gonna just sit back and take whatever crap he's dishing out. And let him know we're watching his ass from now on."

Streeter drew his head back slightly, wincing. "You want me to go threaten this guy and then tail him? Listen, Al, I never do the former and I hate doing the latter. I don't know what you heard about me, but I'm not a hired goon."

At that, Alphonse shot to his feet, elevating himself by all of about eight inches. He threw his hand palm-down toward the desk for emphasis. But he mostly missed, and ended up with his fingers scraping the edge in a feeble tap. "What the hell am I supposed to do? Let this guy walk all over me and my family?" In his excitement, another string of spit laced out of his mouth. "You don't have to threaten him. Just let him know that *we* know and that he better stop that kind of thing. I'm willing to pay you cash up front. Three grand for starters."

The bounty hunter looked at the two of them. Alphonse seemed so shaken and Sheri so concerned. He liked the old man, and his daughter appeared to be genuine enough. Not to mention that three grand was three grand.

"Here's what I'll do," Streeter finally said. "I'll do a background check on Freddy Disanto and Mitch Bosco. And I'll talk to a few people I know at the police department to see if I can get a handle on what they've been up to lately. I'll even ride herd on the fire investigation in Vail. Then, when I get my information, I'll go talk to Disanto and explain what we have. Let him know we can go to the cops with it anytime. No threats and no violence. Just me and him discussing a little situation. Let him know that if he goes cowboy again he'll have to answer to the law."

Alphonse broke into a modest grin. "That'll work for me, Streeter. Just so you dig deep and hard. And if you hear anything bad about Freddy Disanto, do yourself a big favor. Believe it."

5

"I tell you what, Mitchie, it's probably all my fault. If I was really, *really* serious about you torching the right place, I would have sent old man Lucci along with you to point out which house is his."

Freddy Disanto was sitting at his kitchen table, staring at the Friday-morning *Rocky Mountain News.* As he spoke, he shook his head. He didn't look or sound mad, which let Mitch know that he was toasted out of his mind. Carefully, Freddy stroked at the wide expanse of his nose with a middle finger the size of a plump ballpark hot dog as he glanced over the paper to Mitch. Then he nodded.

"Probably would have been a decent idea," Freddy continued softly. "That way, you'd a had someone to talk to on the ride there and back. Musta been a pisser of a lonely trip that time of night."

He paused and nodded again, looking like he was about to smile. Mitch was glad he didn't, because Freddy's smiles had a way of lowering the room temperature a few degrees. Mitch had never seen him this worked up before. With a crazy guy like Freddy Disanto, you knew that cool meant furious and friendly meant watch your backside. Slowly, Freddy set the paper down and sat back in his chair, still staring at the other man. His gentleness made Mitch's eyes narrow in anticipation. He took a quick puff from his Salem 100 before snuffing it out in the ashtray next to his coffee cup. Then he opened his mouth to respond, but quickly shut it. Let Freddy finish first.

Mitch studied the big man for a moment. He'd known the D. for maybe a dozen years, and this was only the second time he had been invited to his home on the southern fringes of Denver. Not much of a place for a roller like Disanto. Two thousand square feet tops, and Mitch had noticed a few Mexicans living on the same block. Guy like the D., Mitch thought he'd be in a high-rise downtown or on Capitol Hill. He figured Disanto pulled down an easy half a mil a year—with most of it unreported to the IRS—what with his restaurants and the assorted numbers-running and bookmaking out of each of them. Combine that with his moving the odd hot products from time to time and what he stood to make on that West Side redevel-opment project and the D. should be sitting pretty by now.

But just look at the man, Mitch thought. Built like a short gorilla wearing an ugly human costume. Barely human. A regular knuckle-dragger all the way. More body hair than a terrier and thick black eyebrows about the size of ski socks. Eyes maybe half a mile apart and a long, cruel mouth. Not that Mitch would mention any of this to the D. personally. You'd have to be nuts to do that. Although he was strictly local and in no way connected to made guys anywhere, Freddy Disanto generally packed a weapon and it was common knowledge that he'd used it at least once. The man would do whatever had to be done to get his way. And he had some dangerous business associates, too. You sure didn't want to screw around with the D. But lately Mitch had been given an opportunity to do a little growing on his own, and even if that meant crossing Freddy Disanto, so be it. "Be realistic about your adversaries," Mitch had read once. "Don't underestimate them or overestimate them. Everyone has a weak spot." That thought kept running through his head as he listened to Freddy's onslaught.

"I suppose I should be glad—huh, Mitchie?" Freddy was now saying as he stood up, coffee cup in hand. He ran his other hand down the front of his wrinkled dress slacks. "Least you ended up in the right ZIP code. Hell, you even made it to within one house of Lucci's. You were very close, you know that, Mitchie?"

Mitch cleared his throat and shifted in his chair. When he looked up at Freddy, he wasn't sure what to say. Whatever it was, he'd probably get hammered. "Look, I thought I wrote it down like you told me, Fred. I'll go back next week and do it right." He paused for a beat and then added, "I'd like it a whole bunch if you didn't call me Mitchie. Makes me sound like a kid."

With that, Freddy quickly and deftly shoved the blond wooden table with his huge right thigh. That pushed it toward Mitch at amazing speed and power. Mitch had been leaning forward, and the edge of the table caught him squarely in the solar plexus, knocking the wind out of him. He made a sudden gurgling sound like he might vomit.

"Shut up, for starters," Freddy hollered. Although his teeth were clenched, his voice was deep enough to cause the glass china-cabinet doors to shudder. "Send you back up there." He shook his head. "I can see it now. In about a month or so, Lucci's place'll be the only one up there left standing. Maybe that should be our new plan. We'll torch all of West Vail and give that little runt something to really think about."

Mitch struggled to compose himself, and glared at Freddy. "I already said I wouldn't charge you for the other night." The words came out staggered and he moved his right hand cautiously over his stomach. "I told you I was sorry about a hundred times."

But Freddy didn't seem to hear him. Instead, he moved to the coffeemaker and poured himself another cup. When he turned back, he was relaxed. "Don't worry about making it up. Some good may come outta this, after all. I'm spreading the word in Lucci's circle that his house was the one we were after. My hunch is the old man already knows he was the target and he's crapping into his Depends by now."

"That doesn't sound like all that great of a idea, does it? Spreading that out there on the street." Mitch sat up. "Could bring the law back to us. To me specifically."

Freddy shook his head and frowned, seemingly confused. "No one's got no proof unless someone saw you up there. *Or* you left a business card. Something stupid like that. You get stupid up there, Mitchie?"

"No." He lit another Salem. "That was one fine job I did. But, still, who needs the police nosing around?"

"I thought you were tight with the DPD these days. Aren't you ratting out Kostas for them?" Freddy glared at Mitch now.

"I got a little cover and they been told by the DA to cut me some slack," Mitch said and then cleared his throat. "But I'm not untouchable. I got them thinking that Teddy Kostas is head of the Mafia, so they gave me breathing room." He could see Freddy's forehead wrinkle in disapproval. "Hell, it was roll on someone or head back downstate for six to nine. I gave 'em Kostas. Who's going to miss that useless fucker?"

"Just so you don't give them anyone else. You follow me, Mitchie?"

"Never you, Freddy," Mitch came back, his voice higher than he intended. "You gotta know that. You think I got a death wish here or what?"

The D. nodded, letting Mitch know the discussion was over. "Just stay in that frame of mind. And stick around town the next week or so. I might need you for some more work on old man Lucci. This arson thing doesn't get him to rethink my proposal, I'll have to get a little rougher."

Mitch stood up. "You know where I'm at, Fred. And you know I'm ready. Always. Like they say, 'Vigilance and fore-sight keep you ahead of the competition.'"

Freddy winced. "Will you give it a rest with all that self-help shit. Godawmighty! You sound like a infomercial. Just stay close to home and be ready to help me give Lucci more grief. That too much to ask, Mitchie?"

"No." He shook his head slowly and stared back at Freddy once more before leaving. It might be just about time for Freddy the D. to get a little of that grief himself, he thought. All that "Mitchie" noise. Mitch knew some people who owed him a favor and he had a pretty good idea what that favor was. Call up the Ramirez Boys. Them screwing over the D. *and* Lucci could really benefit the people in Arizona, Freddy's partners on the West Side development. People Mitch was just about dying to impress.

6

The past three years had been so considerate to Ronnie Taggert that Streeter decided on the spot to start using his minoxidil later that night. Any hint of cheapness in her face, hairdo, or way of dressing was gone. From a distance she looked more mature. Less defensive, clearly sensual. Her hair was still blond and from a bottle. But it was definitely a better bottle, and she wore it shorter and not so teased up. As he walked to her table at a downtown Starbucks shortly after five on Friday afternoon, she smiled broadly at him. He pegged her for about thirty. Less makeup set off her blue eyes better, and several delicate laugh lines made them seem kinder. Not that he'd ever thought of her as mean, still Ronnie had been so streetwise and aggressive that a little softening didn't hurt. He smiled back.

"Hey, gorgeous," she said, and made a movement like she was going to stand. Instead she leaned back. "Glad you made it, but, then, you always do what you say you're going to do." Her head tilted a bit to the side and she gestured casually at the chair across the table, her voice as confident as her posture.

"Ms. Taggert." Streeter slid into the chair and studied her. She wore a pale-blue silk blouse and black pleated silk pants. Obviously expensive and very unlike the tight come-on clothes she used to favor. "You look all growed up. Like you've been to the city." He was quiet for a moment before adding, "You look very nice, Ronnie."

She nodded like someone who'd heard that often. "I was hoping you'd notice," Ronnie replied in an even voice. "You look as good as ever. Still very Streeter-like. How's Frank and the bail-bonds business?"

"Same old. I've been doing more PI work lately and Frank, well, Frank is Frank, as always. Only more so."

"And you?" she asked. "Anything new?"

He shrugged. "A couple more romance disasters, but that's hardly new. Story and I went in the toilet years ago. I started playing the piano, if you can believe that."

"Now, there's a picture. The Terminator does Carnegie Hall."

"Same old Ronnie." He shook his head. "Ever the wiseass."

"If you say so, Tarzan." She paused. "I don't suppose you imagined you'd ever hear from me again."

"I didn't give it much thought. I assumed you were gone for good." He hinted at a smile. "Or, in your case, no good. But I'm glad you called this morning. As long as you're coming through town, we might as well say hi."

"No good, huh?" She considered that." A girl's got to do what a girl's got to do, and I suppose that working for Cooper must have made me look terrible."

"Terrible, no," he responded. "Confused and a shade desperate. But you stood up when it counted and I'll always appreciate your help." He paused. "Speaking of a girl doing what she has to do, what have you been up to all this time? And where?"

"I've been all over the place," Ronnie said, and took a sip of her coffee. "After I left Colorado, I wandered around some," she continued. "Dallas, New Orleans, Atlanta. I finally ended up in Chicago after about a year. I won't bore you with the details. It involved a man who didn't wear his wedding ring and made a lot of empty promises. But Chicago turned out all right. Eventually, I got into your line of work."

Streeter frowned. "Bail bonds? Private detective?"

"Investigations. I met a woman who worked for this PI firm. One of the things they did was investigate spouses and significant others. The firm hired people like me—you know, attractive, with some curb appeal—to do the actual testing."

Streeter nodded. "That would be you, all right. I always thought you had plenty of curb appeal. So you'd go out and try to tempt husbands into straying?"

"Yeah, we were the tempters. We'd put on our tempting clothes and we'd place ourselves where the husbands would notice. You know, like their favorite bar or whatever. Then we'd see if they'd come on to us. It never got farther than the talking stage. At least, not for me. We'd see how hard the men would go for the bait."

"Sounds like unfair entrapment." Streeter sat back and watched her closely. "I mean really. You put a sexy, smiling woman in front of a bored husband who's had a few hoists, what do you expect?"

"About what I got."

"They'd usually go for it?"

"Only about a thousand percent of the time. But you're right. It wasn't exactly a fair test, and there are other ways to find out the same information. I got involved in other kinds of work, too. I ended up getting my PI license from the State of Illinois."

"Are you going to set up a practice in Chicago?" he asked.

She shook her head. "I'm through with that part of the country. Too cold, and I miss Colorado. Which leads me to that business proposition I mentioned in my card." Ronnie carefully set her cup back on the table and bent forward. "There's practically nothing I can't handle in PI work. Plus, I can do most office chores and I know my way around the criminal-justice system, not to mention human nature. Around men, which is mostly who you deal with. I'd like to come to work for you and Frank. He could teach me bail bonds and I could give you a hand with your PI cases. I'm not looking for a huge hourly rate. Just enough to get by, for starters. I'm sure we could work something out where everyone would be happy."

Streeter and Frank had periodically talked about hiring someone to help with the billing and whatnot. This offer surprised him, though. "I don't know, Ronnie. We could use the help around the office. With this PI thing, generally I have enough to keep me going, but there's hardly ever work for more than one person."

"Don't worry about me." She sat back. "I can ride out the slow times, and with your connections and my energy, we'd be bringing in new business." She took a sip of coffee. "You must have an extra little room where I could set up a phone and a desk. I'll print my own cards and you'll only have to pay me out of pocket for the office work. You'd have to do that for any part-timer. As far as the investigations go, give me a referral rate only for what I do. That way, you get paid for my labor and there'd be no danger of you paying me to sit on my hands. We'll make it temporary to start with. Just to see how we all fit together."

Streeter took a drink and noted her perfume. It was Passion. Matched her new image. He set his coffee down. "It could work. But this would be strictly business. Let me think about it. I'm meeting Frank for dinner in a little while. If he goes for it, we'll give it a trial run."

Although Frank Dazzler was looking more *GQ* these days, he was still most comfortable in front of a cold beer and a hunk of steak. Like now, although what he was hearing wasn't going down as well as the Löwenbräu. In his charcoal double-breasted suit and striped power tie, thick combed-back hair, and an earnest face, he was handling aging about as well as anyone could. But the skeptical ex-cop in him had bubbled to the surface when Streeter laid out his proposal.

"I don't know, Street," Frank said as he sawed at his porterhouse. He stopped and looked up. "This Ronnie sounded like more than a small amount of trouble, the last time you dealt with her. And being Thomas Cooper's secretary—or girlfriend or whatever she was—hardly comes as what you'd call a sterling recommendation." He shook his head slowly and winced. "You remember his friends. A regular bunch of psychopaths. You sure you want us to hook up with that crowd again?"

Streeter slowly swirled the Johnnie Walker Red and ice in his glass and studied his slab of ribs. When he left Ronnie, he'd driven down Colfax Avenue, just east of Greek Town, to meet Frank at Bastien's Restaurant, a legendary if shopworn steak house that the bondsman loved. The place was a vintage roundish building cut into several bizarre-shaped rooms on two levels. A wide menu, moderate prices, and stiff drinks. It was a throwback to the old Denver days of neighborhood restaurants heavily done up in someone's version of fifties glitz. Frank's kind of joint.

"We won't be hooking up with that crowd," Streeter finally said. "We'd just be hiring a secretary for you and someone to do legwork for me. All that grunt work I'm so sick of. Mostly, she'll just help you in the office. You've been talking for months now about hiring someone, and besides"—he winked without enthusiasm—"it won't hurt to see a pretty face around the church once in a while. One besides yours, that is."

Frank put down his knife and fork and stared hard at his partner. "That's right. You mentioned she's a knockout. I hope you're not thinking you're going to get a little action on the job by hiring this girl."

"Course not." Streeter took a sip of his Scotch and then set the glass down. "If I wanted to go out with Ronnie I'd just ask her out. Skip all this. Hell, Frank, she's just a kid. All of thirty. *Maybe.* But she's got brains and *cojones* and she's eager to work with us. If she doesn't work out, she's gone. It's not like we're getting married."

"There's a relief," Frank said as he sat back. "If this don't turn out any better than one of your marriages—or longer, for that matter—I'll be pretty disappointed."

"Funny guy."

Frank studied Streeter. "You're generally a pretty good judge of people—your wives aside. I gotta hand you that. So, when you sit there and tell me little Ronnie's okay for the job, I'm inclined to go along with you. I wouldn't mind kicking back a little, myself. As far as your work goes, that's strictly between you and her. But I see you mooning around the place all day or taking three-hour lunches with the new hire, well, we end the whole deal right then and there. We're running a business, not a lonely-hearts club."

Streeter sat up and moved the Scotch glass away from him a few inches with his fingertips. "First of all, I don't 'moon around' anywhere. Secondly, she made it perfectly clear that she's only looking for one thing from us and that thing is work."

"If that's the case, have her come in Monday. About nine." Frank picked up his silverware and focused back on his steak. "I got enough to keep her occupied." He looked back at Streeter for a moment. "How about you? Can little Ronnie help you with that Lucci business?"

Streeter shrugged and picked up a rib without answering. With a crazy bunch like the Luccis, he figured Ronnie might just be able to give him a hand.

7

Getting ready for her first day of work, Ronnie changed clothes several times. First she put on a lightweight red-and-yellow dress. Indian summer had hit Denver over the weekend and it was supposed to be eighty today. But, seeing herself in the mirror, she realized she looked too girlish. Especially given what Streeter had told her on the phone the day before about Frank. The bondsman was strictly old-school. Ladies and gentlemen behaving as such and all that. Not like her last boss. That horny clown thought she was a pleasure perk. But her days of sleeping with the boss had ended when Tom Cooper got himself killed. Now she just wanted work experience and to get a few bucks ahead. Figure out the rest of her life later.

"You want to make a decent first impression on Frank, you play it straight," Streeter had told her. "Dress nice but not like you're too good for the job. Once he gets to know you, then you can loosen up. And be on time. Early would be even better."

No, Ronnie thought as she took the dress off. This one clung to her butt like a hand. Finally, she settled on a denim skirt, almost to her knees, a powder-blue shirt, and a pair of black flats. The outfit said, I'm here to work.

Later, standing in front of the church at quarter to nine, Ronnie studied the neon sign above the door: "Jesus Saves," with the "Jesus" running horizontally and the "Saves" coming down vertically. There was a star above the joint "s" that they shared. The building itself was more neat and updated than she'd expected. Ronnie opened the front door and walked into the large foyer. To the left was the entrance to the "Womyn's Workout Place." Evidently a gym for women who didn't know how to spell or were trying to make some kind of point. She moved quietly down the hall to the right. When she got to Frank's door, she heard what sounded like the music from an old black-and-white movie. Big-band stuff that reminded Ronnie of her father, who used to whistle those tunes. Horn sections of a hundred guys or more, absolutely none of them getting out of line. Subdued drums. She moved to the door and looked inside the room. An older man in a long-sleeved white shirt and a blue tie was sitting at a huge desk studying legal papers. He wore those half-glasses used for reading. His longish hair was dark and fairly shiny. Reminded her of a cool college professor.

"Excuse me," she said as she walked into the room. "Are you Frank Dazzler?"

The man lowered the papers to the desk and looked up, slowly removing the glasses with his left hand. "That's me, darlin'." A confident smile worked its way across his face. Kindly. 'And right now, looking at you, I'm glad I am. I take it you're Ronnie Taggert. Streeter's friend. It's good to finally meet you, Miss Ronnie."

As she approached, Frank stood and extended his hand. He was wearing gray pleated pants. There was a sharp look in his hazel eyes and he was taller and thinner than she expected. She liked being called Miss Ronnie. By him, anyhow. It made her feel special, as did his warm smile. This was a man who genuinely liked women.

"It's nice to meet you, too, Mr. Dazzler," she said as they shook hands.

"Frank's good enough. Mr. Dazzler makes me sound like a Vegas lounge act." Casually he gestured toward a chair on the other side of the desk. When she sat, he dropped back into his chair. He glanced at the clock on a shelf to his left. "I see you believe in being punctual. We're going to get along fine, Miss Ronnie."

Behind Frank and his credenza was a wall of stained glass that gave the place a soft, colorful look. The furniture was more functional than elegant. There was a bookshelf to the right of the desk that was overflowing with paperbacks.

"You're a lot younger-looking than I expected," she said. "Streeter told me that you were old enough to be his father, but I'm guessing older brother. At most. You can't be more than—what?—fifty-five. Fifty-seven, tops."

Frank's eyes opened slightly and he felt himself automatically suck in his stomach. "Aren't you kind?" His voice was soft and he smiled again. "Street's a good man, but he has a way of putting his foot into it from time to time." He took her in as he spoke. Frank pegged her at mid-twenties, but obviously no airhead. She sat tall and proud without giving off any attitude. Like it was just another day at the office, even though she must know this was sort of an interview. Confident women appealed to him, especially ones who looked as nice as Ronnie and underguessed his age by fifteen years. Miss Ronnie here had what they used to call moxie.

"He speaks highly of you, too." Ronnie shot him a smile.

"So, Frank, where do we start? Streeter said you might want me to help get your billing up to date."

"I'm afraid that'll have to wait. Seems I've got an emergency in district court this morning. These things happen." Frank leaned forward as he spoke. "Street should be down here in a minute, and you'll be working with him today." He frowned. "You two figure out your pay for that?"

"I get forty percent of his hourly rate."

Before she could go on, Streeter himself walked into the room. He was wearing one of those shirts with a banded collar that he favored lately. Loose dress slacks and polished shoes. Watching him, Ronnie was glad she'd gone for the look she chose. His face was serious and it took him a few seconds to realize who she was.

"Ronnie," he said as he moved toward the desk. "That's right. Today's the big day. I sure wish I could use you this morning."

Frank stepped in. "If you mean is she free to work for you, this is your lucky day. I'm going down to court, so she's available." With that, he stood up and walked around to the front of the desk.

Ronnie had gotten up as well and was watching the two men. They both seemed a little nervous, obviously not used to having a third person in the room when they worked. She reached out to shake Frank's hand goodbye and he did likewise. He put his left hand on top of their hands as they shook.

"We're not always this slick, Miss Ronnie," he said. "Give us a little time to get used to the new routine." He shot his head back at Streeter. "And don't let him work you too hard." Then he winked at her, turned, and left the room.

Streeter stood in front of her, so Ronnie moved past him to get behind the desk. She lowered herself into Frank's overstuffed chair and looked up at the bounty hunter. He smiled, shook his head, and then sat down in the chair she had just left.

"I knew you'd fit right in, Ronnie, but I didn't think you'd take over this soon."

"I'm just getting comfortable, Street." She watched for a reaction. "You mind if I call you that? I like the way it sounds when Frank says it."

"That's okay with me, but don't expect me to call you Miss Ronnie and don't get too comfortable. You're going to be running around town most of the morning."

"Doing what?"

Streeter looked at the desktop and pointed to a legal pad near the phone. "You better write this down. We've got to check out a few people for a PI case I picked up last week. Have you ever heard of an Alphonse Lucci?"

Ronnie shook her head and grabbed the pad and a Bic pen. "Should I have?"

"Probably not. Have you ever been to Motor Vehicles to check driving records?"

"A couple of times. For Cooper."

"Good. Go out there this morning and get Alphonse Lucci's driving history. L-U-C-C-I. DMV usually wants to know the person's date of birth, but I don't have one. I'd say he's about seventy. Then get the histories for a Mitch Bosco, he's early forties, and a Fred Disanto. B-O-S-C-O and D-I-S-A-N-T-O. Disanto's a little older—about my age or more. Then head on over to the courthouse and look up the criminal and civil records for all of those guys. That's the Denver courthouse, second floor. Just ask someone where the records room is."

"I know it." She looked up from the pad. "Do you want copies of everything?"

"All felonies and any misdemeanors that seem interesting. This is only for my information, so you don't have to copy every page. Just the complaints and how the case was resolved. Same thing with any interesting civil suits."

Ronnie was watching him closely. "How much older than forty are you?"

Streeter rolled his eyes. "Not much. Disanto could be in his late forties. Fifty, even."

"What's this all about?"

"We work for Al and his daughter. Sheri Lucci. That's Sheri with an 'i.' Like a model or a hairdresser. Check her out, too." He stood up. "They have reason to believe that Bosco and Disanto are trying to hurt them. They think that Disanto ordered a fire at the house next to theirs in Vail. It's a long story."

"Do you usually investigate your clients?" Ronnie also stood up, holding the legal pad close to her as she did.

"No. But this is one weird situation and I heard that Al hasn't always operated above the law." He glanced at the clock. "I'll be downtown the rest of the morning, and then I've got a few things to take care of this afternoon. You've got enough work to keep you busy for a while, and considering you'll be going at thirty-five an hour, you'll make some money today. Meet me back here in the morning. Let's shoot for eight-thirty this time."

"About how old is this Sheri?" Ronnie moved from behind the desk.

"Hell, she's just a kid. Can't be more than forty."

8

Freddy Disanto had been winning big all night, which happened about as often as a Kennedy acting like a gentleman. He looked at the chunky stack of money in front of him and figured he was up close to five grand. Had to be his best night ever. Freddy the D. had never seen so many similar faces on his cards. One thing for sure, they were better-looking than the six faces sitting around the table. At forty-seven, Freddy was way younger than the rest of the guys playing five-card draw. But they could handle their cards. Freddy the D. had to give them that. Even with the hands he was catching tonight, he still couldn't pull away more than a couple hundred bucks each hand. These old guys hung on to their money like it was part of their skin. The D. had to give them that.

He glanced at his host. Damned Cheese Man hopping around the table like the carpet was on fire. Not playing. Just studying everyone without looking directly at their cards.

Freddy knew that Alphonse Lucci had *never* liked him, particularly since the D. had started in on him a few months earlier about buying his pizza joint. The relationship between the two had gone from bad to horrible after that. But Alphonse let him keep playing out of habit, seeing as how Freddy had been pretty much of a regular there for almost fifteen years. Even during the time when Freddy's father went away. That and because the D. normally lost big. But tonight was different. Alphonse seemed ready to blow a gasket. Freddy the D. liked that, because he simply hated the old man. Little schmuck Lucci in his maroon velvet smoking jacket, his tiny head poking up from the oversized garment like he was a scared turtle. Glasses thick as ashtrays, and the frames so big it looked like his head couldn't support them. But tonight even Freddy the D. didn't mind him all that much. He was winning big.

The other players chewed their cigars and grumbled, not giving one good rip how Freddy Disanto and the Cheese Man were getting along. All they knew was that most of their money was drifting toward Freddy's end of the table, and that had never happened before. They were certain that he was too stupid to cheat, so they chalked it up to blind luck. If they could keep him playing long enough, they knew that he'd piss it away eventually. That the money would start rolling back their way sooner or later. Hell, it was only a little after ten. By midnight things should be back the way they were supposed to be.

Only one of the Ramirez Boys was actually named Ramirez. That would be Manny. The other two "boys" were Neal Ringo and Albert Hepp. But the three of them had been inseparable since they'd first met in the fourth grade—up in Cheyenne, twenty years earlier—and Manny had always been the leader. He was the only one who possessed what might be called brains and judgment. Neal and Albert were more or less extensions of Manny. Like his arms. They did whatever he said with a minimum amount of lip. Neither of them ever came up with an independent idea. In fact, by the time they'd made it to high school, Manny had earned the nickname Top Cat. After the old cartoon character cat that had a crew of numb nuts to carry out his every harebrained scheme. Only Manny's schemes were more vicious and profitable than stupid. Not that they were ever what you'd call complex. To these three the equation was simple: you had a gun, you had access to money. The Ramirez Boys always had plenty of guns, and this plan was about as basic as you could get.

"It's all set up, Manny," Mitch Bosco had told him over the phone on Saturday. "All laid out for you. You know the location and the take'll just be sitting there to be scooped up. Wear some masks and scare the crap out of them. Guys this old, that shouldn't be tough. They'll be playing cards and I know for a fact they won't be armed. No one's ever had the balls to try and take this game out. Not until now."

Manny listened on the other end, liking the job pretty well. It would kill two birds with one stone. First, it would even the score with Bosco. Mitch had bailed Manny's butt out of a jam a few months earlier, when he helped him unload some hot merchandise to a buyer in New Mexico. And, second, there was money to be made.

"What's our end in all this?" Manny had asked. "And how much we have to turn over to you when we're done, huh?"

"That's the beauty of it," Mitch had answered. "For you, anyhow. Your end is whatever's in the pot. You don't owe me a thing."

Manny frowned and briefly glanced at the receiver in his hand. "Why's that?"

"Because I've got my own reasons for this thing happening and you don't have to know nothing about that. Just promise me one thing. If you ever get in a spot where someone asks you who turned you on to this game, tell them it was some old Italian dude from Denver. He was just a voice on the phone and that's all you know." He paused. "In fact, that's all that crew of yours should hear. You and me are the only ones need to know about this. You promise me that and we're even. Not to mention you're ahead a few grand."

That didn't sound any more than reasonable to Manny. Still. "So you set this up and all you want out of it is nothing? No money?"

"I get out of it what I get out of it and that's all you gotta know."

"Okay. I'm there." A few minutes of work for maybe ten grand in small bills. All of it belonging to a few old West Denver wops. Might be worth the ninety-minute drive down to the city.

Now, as he moved the pickup truck smoothly down I-25 with the Denver skyline coming into view to the south, Manny was again going through the details with Neal and Albert.

"There's an alley right behind the store or whatever it is," Manny was saying. He shot a glance to his right. Neal looked jumpy from the coke he'd been packing up his nose all night. But that was okay. That idiot cowboy always worked better with half a gram in his bloodstream. Be all right just so nobody inside made any quick moves. Albert, well, he was another story. The fat man leaned against the passenger's door, holding a forty of Mickey's Malt Liquor in a brown paper bag. His eyes were almost shut; his face was flat as a shovel. About as expressive, too. Albert looked ready for jack shit. "Our contact man said the door back there is always left open so them humps can come and go as they please," Manny continued. "This game's been played there every Monday night for the past hunnert years or so, and they don't worry about security."

"Big mistake," Albert said, suddenly looking happy as only the seriously stupid can.

"That's damned straight, Bubba," Manny said to the steering wheel. "We're in and out in three minutes. Tops. I do the talking, you hold 'em down." He paused and looked to his right again. "And you, Albert. You cover the back door. Nobody comes in while we're there. You can handle that, huh?"

Albert nodded once, his eyes now showing only the tiniest flicker of comprehension.

Freddy the D. was leaning hard on his huge elbows, which were planted on the table and locked into a V. Both of his hands were holding his just-dealt cards tight and close to his face. When the three men burst in through the back door, Freddy barely noticed them, even though he was facing their direction. He was just sort of aware of motion across the room. It was Art, sitting to Freddy's left, who first noticed the men. Art, who was maybe the oldest man there and who played cards with an oxygen tank pumping air into his nostrils as he chewed an unlit cigar. His head jerked back and the stogie dropped into his lap. That's what Freddy the D. noticed first. Then he looked to where old Art's eyes were riveted. Freddy frowned and automatically started to move his six-foot-three-inch frame up and out of his chair.

"Sit the fuck down!" Manny yelled at him while walking toward the table, his chrome nine-mil held in both hands, Dirty Harry style.

Freddy the D. was no genius, but he could see right off that the nine pointed at his head beat his pair of kings by a mile. So he dropped his cards as he lowered himself back into his chair. Silently, he wondered if he could get to the tiny .22 he had taped to his left ankle without the jerk in the cheap Nixon mask noticing. He quickly realized that the answer was no. Not with the guy focusing right on him like that.

Manny could feel his face sweating wildly under the plastic mask. His read was that the big dark guy he'd just yelled at was the only one who could give him any trouble. The rest of the players looked harmless, like a batch of shriveled apples sitting around waiting to be swept away. So Manny kept his gun on the big man while Neal, wearing an identical Nixon mask, paced behind him with his sawed-off shotgun sweeping the table. Somewhere in back of Neal, Albert was leaning against the doorframe. Albert had gone with a hockey goalie's face mask for the evening, and he was casually dividing his attention between the card table and the outside world in the alley.

"Everyone, just stay calm and you might make it out of here alive!" Manny yelled. He noticed one of the old guys, a small pale man in a shiny red bathrobe, was standing off to the left of the table. "Get over there, you little goof," he screamed at him while jerking the gun in the direction of the card players.

"Wha' the hell?" one of the old men asked loudly from the table. "Who are you people?"

Manny glanced at the man, the one sitting next to the young guy and sporting tubes running out of his nose into a tank.

"We're the people robbing you, huh?" Manny responded. "You just worry about us shooting you up." He paused and waved his gun at the wall across from the door. "Everybody! Empty your pockets on the table and then go over there and lie on the floor. Facedown. That way my man here"—he gestured to Neal—"won't have to shoot you up. You do what I say, huh?"

When nobody budged and the old men just kept looking at each other frowning, Manny aimed his nine at the wall behind the big man and fired a round. The gun seemed to explode in the small room, and the plywood wall smoldered where the bullet hit it. Got the old guys' attention real good, too. In unison they all sort of hopped in their chairs and then leaned forward, reaching for their pockets. As they did, Neal pulled a soiled pillowcase from his back pocket and moved over to the table. The card players emptied their pockets. So did Al Lucci. The only one who didn't respond was Freddy the D. He just sat there glaring at Manny, too pissed to do anything. Holding his nine in one hand now, Manny walked to the table and stood right behind the D. Then he popped Freddy on the top of the head with the bottom of the gun grip. It was only a few inches above Freddy's skull when it came down, but it hit him with remarkable force. That caused Freddy's head to fly toward the table. A thick tear broke out in the corner of one eye.

"I'm talking to you, too, asshole!" Manny screamed. "The next shot goes into your head, you don't do what I say."

Freddy the D. felt like he was hit with a hammer, which clearly took most of the fight out of him. He struggled not to cry anymore and instead just stood up and emptied his pockets. He glanced around the table and saw seven small assorted piles of keys on gold chains, handkerchiefs, combs, wads of cash, and wallets. He made his own little stack in front of him and then moved around the chair to where the other men were struggling to lie on the floor. It looked like a yoga class at an old folks' home. The D. moved a couple feet from the others and then dropped himself to the floor. The thought of all the money he was losing made him want to cry more than the bang on the head had.

"That's good," Manny said, his voice lower than before. "We don't want no dead old wops here." He turned to watch Neal scooping up everything valuable from the table. Even the quick glance told Manny that Mitch Bosco's estimate of ten thousand dollars was pretty accurate. Had to be at least that going into the filthy pillowcase. Behind Neal, he could see Albert watching, too, and yawning like the whole thing was boring him half to death. Then Manny looked back at the old men, who by now were all on the floor with their heads close to the wall.

"Facedown!" His voice rose. "All of you!"

The eight men more or less complied. The whack on the head apparently had put the big guy in the right frame of mind, because he now had his face almost buried in the thick carpet. When he could see that Neal was finished, Manny started backpedaling toward the door. As they both reached where Albert stood, they were about eight feet from the round table, with the card players another few feet beyond that. Manny glanced at his watch. They'd been there less than three minutes. Excellent. He looked back once more at the men on the floor. But before he could say anything else, Albert spoke up.

"Let's go, Manny," he said in a voice that echoed loudly through the room.

Mother of God, Manny thought. The hell was that all about? He spun and glared at Albert through his plastic Nixon face. The fat man at the door just stood there, his mouth dropping open under his mask. Neal was looking at Albert as well. Manny tapped Neal on the shoulder with his free hand. Then Manny pointed to the wall above the card players and said softly, "Make some more noise but don't go hitting no one."

Neal Ringo took a couple of quick steps toward the men and raised his shotgun to a few inches above his waist, right hand on the trigger, left on the base of the barrel. Then he unloaded a blast into the plywood wall, about three feet over the prone men. It sounded as though a garbage truck had fallen off the roof. Manny was sure some of the old guys would never hear very well again, and he hoped it would confuse all of them enough so they'd forget his name. With that, the Ramirez Boys backed out of the room. Manny slammed the door behind them, and they were in the idling pickup truck within seconds after that.

Still lying there facedown even after the door shut, Freddy Disanto realized two things. One: that was Manny Ramirez and his crew who had just left the room. Two: he'd pissed in his pants when the shotgun went off.

9

"You were right about all of them having dirt under their nails." Ronnie set a file folder on the desk and looked at Streeter and Frank. "Even your friend Sheri Lucci. Sheri with an 'i.' "

"What do you mean, she's dirty?" Frank asked.

"Not dirty, just some problems." Ronnie shrugged. "Apparently she likes to drive fast, and fourteen years ago she was charged with assault and battery. Seems she took a pipe wrench to her ex-husband and banged him up a little. I gather from the files that they had a stormy marriage. The assault charge got reduced to a misdemeanor and she pleaded out. Six months' probation." She paused. "They were divorced for about two years before the incident occurred, so she must have a hard time letting go."

Streeter could picture Sheri doing that. Her old man's daughter through and through. He looked at Ronnie. "How about the rest of them?"

She pointed to the file. "It's all in there. Mitch Bosco likes to drink. Lost his license eight years ago for DUI. Got it back a while ago. Obviously, a career criminal. He's done county time for"—she glanced down at the notebook in her lap—"burglary, possession of stolen goods, two assaults, and more burglary. State time at Buena Vista for assault with a deadly weapon and—surprise, surprise—attempted arson."

"That fits," Frank said.

"Mr. Disanto," Ronnie continued. "An interesting man. His driving record is clean, but he's been charged with statutory rape, and attempting to intimidate a witness. Twice. Got probation every time. One count of extortion, too, but it was dismissed. He *did* do some federal time a few years back for receiving stolen goods." Her eyebrows shot up. "I checked federal court, too. Seemed like a light sentence for what-all he was into at the time. Then there's civil court. He's been involved in a ton of suits over money, and with a former employee suing him about back wages. Most of it just went away. I gather either he has one terrific lawyer or he's a very persuasive man." She leaned closer to Streeter. "By the way, he's forty-seven."

"What about Alphonse?" Streeter ignored the age business.

"He's a funny one, too." Ronnie looked down at her pad. "He had his license suspended a few years ago on points. He's got sort of a rap sheet, but it reads more like a teenager's. Disorderly conduct: urination." She looked up and shook her head. "Seems he's got a weak bladder and he's prone to relieving himself in the nearest alley or wherever's convenient." Then she focused on the pad again. "There's some gambling arrests, too. Probation each time. And one count of theft by receiving in '86." She looked up at the two men. "Nothing in federal court, and just a lot of small stuff in civil court. All of it relating to his restaurants."

"Sounds like your Alphonse Lucci's not much of a player," Frank said.

"Nice touch, hitting federal court," Streeter told Ronnie. Then he turned to Frank. "None of them are very big time. I did a computer sweep of the state and it seems these guys never leave town. There was nothing outside of Denver except for Bosco. He's been charged with theft by receiving in Adams County a while ago. Pleaded it way down. Also, I talked to the people investigating the Vail arson and they've got nothing. Strictly professional. No witnesses, no motive. Might as well forget that one unless Sheri comes forward, which she's not going to do."

He glanced back at Ronnie. "Evidently, Bosco's not a complete fool. I talked to an old friend of mine at Denver Crimes Against Persons. Detective Carey. He's heard of Bosco, and Disanto's name rang a bell, too. He's going to do an NCIC on them to see if they have any problems out of state. But the bottom line is we're dealing with two rotten guys here in Freddy and Mitch. They don't seem to be killers exactly, and they're not connected to the really big boys—no Mafia or anything like that. Both are strictly local and fairly small-time. But if they're going for arson, they're dangerous. And they're motivated. Al said Freddy has a lot on the line with this condo project. Plus, there's that business between Lucci and Freddy's father. Carey told me that little Al held out for all of ten or twelve seconds before he rolled Disanto's old man to save his own butt."

Streeter adjusted himself in his chair. "Carey also said he's heard gossip lately in the department about Bosco. Something to do with the DA's office. That's all he knows."

"Maybe he's paying people off." Frank leaned forward, frowning.

"Doubtful."

"Maybe he's under investigation himself," the bondsman offered.

"We can only hope," Streeter responded.

"Or he's a snitch," Ronnie interjected.

They both looked at her. "It's possible," Streeter said. "But how that figures into all this is beyond me. Carey said he'd do a little snooping but I'm not holding my breath on that."

Ronnie cleared her throat. "You know, while I was down at the courthouse, I thought I might as well check your divorce history, too, Street. Seems you've had a little difficulty in that area. By the way, I can see why you don't use your first name. Anyhow, they practically have a whole Streeter wing over there. Four times?"

Frank let out a quick grunt that passed as a laugh and Streeter frowned. "You checked out my divorces?"

Ronnie shrugged and flashed a grin. "I didn't bill you for the time, Tarzan. Anyhow, I'd suggest a little marriage counseling before you take any more walks down the aisle. The fourth one lasted—what?—sixteen months?"

Streeter frowned. "Well, I'm sure it couldn't compare to that beautiful thing you and Tom Cooper had going. That was a regular union made in heaven."

Ronnie kept smiling and was about to say something when the phone rang. She leaned forward, keeping eye contact with him, and picked up the receiver.

"Bail Bonds," she said, and waited. Finally, "I'll see if I can find him. May I say who's calling?" Then she put her hand over the mouthpiece. "It's Al Lucci."

Streeter grabbed the phone. "Hello."

"Yeah, hi there, Streeter. It's Al. We gotta talk."

"So talk."

"I don't know where to start. Normally I'd say Disanto's

up to his old tricks, but he was one of the guys that got his ass kicked over here."

"What are you talking about? This isn't another fire, is it?"

"I almost wish, but no." Al coughed loudly into the phone. "Last night a few of us boys were playing a little poker over here, down the hall from my office. About eleven or so, these three assholes wearing masks come storming in and start shooting up the walls. No one got hit, but they took us down for ten, twelve grand along with assorted personal valuables and such."

"Disanto did that?"

"Not likely, seeing as how he was one of the boys that got taken down. He was playing with us when it happened. Even took a good rap to the head. If this was his plan, the man's a masochist."

"He was hurt?"

"He'll live." Al coughed again. "One of the gunmen tapped him on the noodle to get his attention. You know, get his mind right. Then they took everything in the room that resembled money, including all of Disanto's cash, which was considerable. My only consolation is that, on the first night Disanto's ahead in maybe four years, he gets it all ripped off before he can spend a penny."

"You have any idea who did it?"

"Just about certain. Guy name of Manny Ramirez and his crew. They're from up in Wyoming, and they come down here once in a while to pull shit like this. But the Ramirez Boys are a bunch a bugs and they couldn't a figured this out on their own. I tell you Streeter, I got no idea in hell who set it up."

"Maybe you should pick a new set of friends," Streeter said. Al made a small grunting noise but didn't say anything. "What did the police say?" Streeter asked.

"I can't go to them with this. That game was about as legal as the robbery."

"So what do you want me to do, Al?"

"What I *really* want you to do is throw this son of a bitch Disanto off Lookout Mountain. He's foremost on my mind, and now he's giving me even more crap because I let this thing happen at my joint. I also wouldn't mind if you found out who put Ramirez and his idiots up to that stunt." His voice softened. "But it's mainly the D. Get him off my back, Streeter. I'm too old for this. I can't take much more of it."

"How about if I drop by later and we'll see what we can come up with?"

"Tomorrow. First thing in the morning. Today, I gotta deal with the guys from last night. Calm them down some."

"Okay. I'll be over at ten in the morning."

"Do that." He paused. "And Streeter?"

"Yeah."

"Sheri says hi."

10

Albert Hepp figured that from now on he could live just fine without Manny Ramirez telling him what to do every few minutes. But, then, Albert always was a very dumb man. No one who ever talked to him for more than a minute or so would argue with that.

"Your balls are a lot bigger than your brains, *amigo*," Manny had yelled at him that afternoon, just before he and Neal split town. "And that ain't no real compliment to your balls, either. You stick around here, them crazy guineas gonna come by and put the hurt on you real good, huh? Bad enough you go and tell them who we are. Yell my name out like that when we're leaving. But now you sticking around like this, it makes no sense."

"There's lots of guys named Manny," Albert came back. "How they gonna know it was you I was talking about?"

Manny shook his head and got into the pickup truck. He looked once more at the fat man standing on the curb in downtown Cheyenne, clutching the neck of an unopened bottle of malt liquor in a brown paper bag. Albert's face displayed its usual utter lack of anything. Two small eyes, close together over a nose crooked as a Cheeto. Mouth perpetually open about an inch. Manny wondered if Albert's lips had ever touched. Ever. "Your last chance, man. You don't come now, you're on your own."

"Where you headed?" Albert switched his weight to his right leg and scratched idly at his crotch.

Manny thought for a moment and then glanced at Neal, sitting next to the passenger's door. He winked and turned back to Albert. "Canada. No one'll look up there. I got a cousin in Montreal. We'll lay low at his place until this all blows over. You coming, huh?"

"No," Albert said, switching his weight back to the other leg. "And I mean *fuck* no. Too cold up there."

"Suit yourself, huh?" With that, Manny shoved the truck into first gear and pulled away from the curb without looking back. When he'd gone about half a block, he turned to Neal again. "Think he'll remember that my cousin lives in New Orleans?"

"Most the time, he don't remember that the President lives in Washington, D.C.," Neal responded. "You said Canada, he's thinking Canada."

Now, as Albert Hepp watched a *Honeymooners* repeat in Glenda's mobile home, he was polishing off yet another forty. He had to take a leak, but he didn't feel like walking all the way to the bathroom in the rear, next to the bedroom. He glanced down at the bottle in his hands and briefly thought about pissing into it. But he could feel there was still a couple inches of brew in there and he didn't want to waste it. He looked over at the door, about four feet from the couch, and decided he'd urinate off the side porch. Hell, it was after one o'clock on Wednesday morning. Idiot neighbors would all be asleep. Albert stood up, his bathrobe shifting open as he did. He was wearing only a pair of green plaid boxer shorts and yellow socks underneath it. He took one more look down the hall, toward where Glenda was sleeping. Good old Glenda. Might be built like a bookshelf and shy a tooth or two, but, man oh man, she could outcook and outscrew any woman in the whole state of Wyoming. Satisfied she was still asleep, Albert moved to the door and opened it.

Outside, the night was so dark that it took his eyes a while to adjust to it. Before they completely did, he felt a huge hand gripping the front collar of his bathrobe. He opened his mouth to say something, but the hand yanked hard at his robe and jerked his whole body onto the little wooden deck. The force of the pull was so strong that Albert flew out the door and moved straight ahead about five feet. His stomach, at about the level of his belly button, rammed into the metal railing. He bounced hard off of it and back onto the deck, losing his footing as he did. Albert slammed down onto his back, the rear of his head hitting the bottom of the door-frame he had just left.

His arm, the hand still holding the bottle of malt liquor, flew off to the side, and the bagged bottle hit the wall of the trailer, causing a muffled crash. Albert himself let out an abrupt scream, nearly going unconscious. Before he could move, he felt someone grab his ankles and pull him toward the edge of the porch and under the metal railing. His head lifted slightly to see a man standing on the ground and pulling him out. This clearly was one strong man: he yanked the 238-pound Albert Hepp straight out and over the edge of the deck. Albert, dazed, could feel air beneath himself for a second, and then his backside landed on the ground, about three and a half feet below the edge of the deck. Knocked the wind out of him so fast that he could only let out a swift, dull "ugggh."

He was nearly unconscious as he lay there, wondering how one man could get around the porch so fast and move him out there like that. Then he became aware of the guy kneeling over him. He was now holding Albert's robe front again in his giant paw. Blinking hard several times, Albert could hear the man say, "Hey, shit-for-brains. You remember me?"

At that moment Albert didn't actually remember how many toes he had. He shook his head and muttered, "Naw."

Apparently that wasn't much of an answer, because the guy's fist shot into Albert's nose, breaking it. Albert thought how it sounded like someone taking a step onto frozen snow.

"You stopped by our little card game last night," the man continued. "That coming back to you now?"

Albert could feel his bathrobe bunched up under his upper back. He was aware that his huge gut was exposed to the man kneeling next to him and that a warm blast of piss had come out of him, short but hard, when he hit the ground. Card game? Of course. It finally dawned on him why this was happening.

"You," was all he could get out. He still had no idea who the guy was.

"Damned right it's me."

The man's voice sounded slightly familiar now, and Albert assumed it was the big, younger guy from the poker game. The one who looked like he could crush cinderblocks in his bare hands, no sweat.

"I'm Freddy Disanto," the voice continued. "Definitely not the guy you want all mad at you like this." He paused. "Where are your two girlfriends?"

Albert frowned. "Glenda?"

Freddy the D.'s fist came back down into his face, this time landed mostly on Albert's lower jaw. Another sound of frozen snow. "Who the hell is that? I'm talking about Manny and Ringo. Where are they?"

Albert's mind gave him permission to give up his friends before Freddy had even finished asking. "Canada. Montreal. Manny's cousin lives up there."

"What's the cousin's name?"

"Ramirez," Albert said.

"I could guess that much, jerkoff. What's the first name?"

"I 'unno."

"You're very loyal," Freddy the D. came back. "That's so admirable." He threw another fist into Albert's jaw.

"But you asked!" Albert's voice rose to a whine.

"What a pig." Freddy paused. "Who put you morons up to that move?"

"Manny."

Freddy's eyes rolled in the darkness. "I mean, who put *Manny* up to it?"

Albert frowned, desperately trying to remember the man's name. He had no idea. All Manny had told him and Neal was that an Italian from Denver called him and set it up. An old guy, no names. Seeing as how all he cared about was the money, Albert hadn't ask anything beyond that. "Some guy phoned Manny from Denver. All I know was he was a wop and that's that. Some old guy."

"Lucci?" Freddy the D. moved his head back slightly. "Al Lucci?"

"Could be. I never heard the name." He paused, figuring it was better to be as helpful as possible. "Yeah, I think that's it."

Freddy the D. let go of the bathrobe and stood up. He stared down at Albert, who lay there without moving except for the broad up and down of his chest and belly as he breathed. Freddy sniffed the air.

"You pissed in your pants, didn't you?" he asked the man on the ground.

"I think so," Albert said, still pretty confused.

Freddy the D. put his right hand into his coat pocket and pulled out a handgun with a long silencer attached. Albert couldn't exactly make it out to be a gun, but his frown deepened. Even if he wasn't sure what Freddy was holding in the darkness, he could guess it wasn't good news. He opened his mouth to say something, anything that might calm the man down. He thought about repeating the Canada business, but that didn't seem to make much sense. Then he thought about calling out for Glenda. Like that would do him any good. Just get her into trouble. Before he could move or say anything, the gun went off. Twice. Barely as loud as a book slamming shut. Albert's body jolted a couple of times and then he was still.

Staring silently at the fat body for a moment, Freddy the D. thought of Alphonse Lucci. That feeble old man had knocked off his own card game just to cause Freddy trouble. He'd pay for that move. Time to turn up the heat on Lucci, the D. reasoned. Talk to Mitchie about it when you get back to Denver. Then he thought of Manny Ramirez and his other partner. And then Lucci again. He studied the body at his feet. This should get the right message to all three of those guys. Especially Lucci. The other two, who cared.

"No way I'm going up to Canada this time of year," the D. said softly to no one in particular. Way too cold, he thought. And, hell, it was only a stupid card game.

With that, he turned and walked back to his car.

11

When Streeter walked into the office that Wednesday morning, Alphonse Lucci was shivering like a wet spaniel. His pale face looked smaller than usual behind his glasses. Sheri was standing over his left shoulder, and they were looking at a fax sheet on top of the desk. As Streeter approached, the Luccis looked up. Al's head bobbed twice in what Streeter interpreted to be nerves.

"Streeter," Al said, glancing down at the desk again. "You gotta read this fax I just got." He shook his head and looked back up. "A fax it is nowadays. You believe that?"

Streeter got to the desk and looked down. "What's it about?"

"Freddy Disanto," Sheri said. "He's going off the deep end."

Streeter glanced up at her. Sheri was wearing a little more makeup than the first time he'd met her. She was looking closely at him, and he wondered if he detected the trace of a smile on her face. "How so?" he asked her.

"You read this sheet and tell me," Alphonse stepped in. "Looks to me like he already killed one of the robbers from the other night and he claims that the other two left the country."

Streeter picked up the fax sheet. It was typed out, sloppy, and with only a casual interest in grammar and spelling. But the message seemed fairly clear:

> I understand that one of the punks who visited your place Monday night is no longer with us. His body was found early this morning in Cheyenne. I also understand that the other two perps are no longer residing in this particular country for fear of having the same thing happen to them. A fairly healthy notion since I'm not thrilled with being jerked around like we were by them.

"He faxed you what amounts to nearly a confession." Streeter looked at both of them.

"That would be my assumption," the old man said. "With a head case like the D., it probably didn't register what he was doing. But how else did he know about that goofus getting whacked up there in Cheyenne? It had to be him. I made some calls to a guy I know up there and it seems that one Albert Hepp was found this morning shot to death outside a trailer. Albert was a close associate of Manny Ramirez."

Streeter looked back at the sheet and continued reading.

"I also want you to know that I expect to be reimbursed for the five grand or so these individuals took off of me Monday night. Your game, your job to see it's safe. Not to mention that the dead man in Wyoming was known to tell people that it was you who hired him. D."

"What the hell does that mean?" Streeter asked when he finished reading. "You get robbed and then you're held liable to pay Disanto for his losses. He's trying to put this thing with the Ramirez Boys on you?"

"So it would seem," Al said sadly. "This Hepp must a said I hired them. A course, I imagine he was under a great deal a stress and pressure at the time he made that little confession. But, still, why would he finger me? I mean, I know some heavy people around town, but this . . ." The old man shook his tiny head and looked down at his empty desktop.

Sheri rolled her eyes. "Sure you do." She said. "You're a regular organized-crime kingpin."

The old man's head jerked up at that. "I *know* people," he said hoarsely, with all the pride he could muster.

"Right." Sheri turned to Streeter. "He had one second cousin who lived in New Jersey and hung out with a few wise guys. That's exactly who he knows. And that cousin's been dead for nine years now." She glanced back at Alphonse. "You don't know squat and it's time you admit it."

The little man stared off but said nothing at first. "Maybe so, but we gotta find out who set up that robbery. I, personally, don't have a clue."

"We've got more important things to deal with here," the bounty hunter said. "First off, are you going to show this to the police?"

They both shook their heads in unison. "What for?" Al asked. "All it says is 'D.' That can't be traced to Freddy. Not to mention that he doesn't come right out and actually admit to anything."

"You're right about that," Streeter said. "If Disanto killed Hepp, that means he's capable of anything. And if he's blaming you for hiring Ramirez, then he's capable of doing anything to you. Which means we've got to deal with Freddy boy. Fast. I'd also like to find out exactly who it was that actually did hire Manny and his crew. That's essential."

"You're right about Disanto," Al said, saliva forming on

the corners of his mouth. "Those rumors about him must be true. Either he did this Wyoming thing or he sent someone like Bosco up to do it. I've got to get him some money to make good for the other night." He homed in on Streeter. "And you've got to give me some breathing room here. This guy's making me mental."

Streeter shook his head. "You're not paying Disanto a penny. That would be like admitting you set up the robbery." He paused for a long moment. "Have you given any more thought to selling out to him?"

"Yeah," the old man said. "But it ain't gonna happen, Streeter. I'd rather get blown away than break my word to my father." He stiffened slightly. "And I'm not gonna let this mutt dictate my life to me."

"Well, if that's the way you want to play it, then we confront Disanto and let him know the score." Streeter paced slowly in front of the desk. "I want to go talk to Freddy and I want to do it fast. Hopefully today. Tomorrow at the latest. Do you have any idea where's the best place to get to him? And I wouldn't mind a suggestion or two on how I should approach the man."

"Tomorrow's Thursday," Al said. "I know for a fact that he eats lunch every Thursday at Pagliacci's. I know people who've met him there once or twice." He blinked at Streeter. "You know the place? It's over on 33rd, near the freeway."

The bounty hunter nodded.

"Good," Alphonse continued. "He's usually alone. Guy like Fred don't have much use for bodyguards or that kind of thing. I think he keeps a girl near there and he visits her after he's done eating. Anyhow, you get over there a few minutes before noon, when he's just sitting down. That's our best move."

"Sounds okay. I'll let him know that your feelings on the sale are final and that you had nothing to do with the robbery," Streeter said. "Then I'll also let him know we know about the whole Vail business and that you're feeling very uncomfortable about the entire situation. I'll let him know that we've been talking to the police about all of it, including Cheyenne, and they're getting interested in him. That's mostly BS, but it wouldn't hurt to have Disanto thinking along those lines. And, finally, I'll let him know that I'm keeping a close watch on you and your family from now on. We've got to get this guy on the defensive."

"You'll be watching us?" Sheri asked.

He looked at her. "Probably not much, but more than before."

The two held eye contact for a moment, so Alphonse spoke up. "You'll want to be firm with the D., but don't be getting into his face none." The old man nodded wisely. "Freddy the D. wouldn't take to that kind of thing. He's one of those guys that walks around cocked and ready to go off at all times."

Streeter nodded. "What does he look like?"

Alphonse smiled. "Picture a big pit bull in a silk suit and a lousy haircut. And I'm being generous here, Streeter. You'll know him. No neck to speak of and yellow eyeballs. And he'll probably be the only one in the joint eating with his fingers. The D. is no beauty, and he's even a little taller than you. Broader, too, and we're not talking baby fat here." Then he frowned. "Freddy's barely civilized and he's got the pain threshold of a asphalt highway."

"That's very encouraging," the bounty hunter said. "It's a public place, and he's not likely to pull anything there if I don't get too stiff with him."

No one spoke for a long time. The Luccis focused on the fax again, and Streeter was thinking about meeting Freddy the next day. Finally, Alphonse looked up. "You find out anything more on Mitch Bosco? Your cop friend any help?"

"Something's going on between him and the police," Streeter said. "My source, Carey, tells me he hears that Bosco's helping the police with something. I met Carey last night for beers and he claims he doesn't know anything more than that. And he's not going to know anything more in the future, either. He made it clear to me that whatever Bosco's doing with the cops is being kept quiet." He paused. "I think it would be a good idea if I followed Bosco around a little. Might not even hurt if he knew I was doing it. That way he could get the word back to Disanto. Like I said, I want Freddy on the defensive. I keep a slow, steady flame under these two and something's bound to shake out for us."

"That could get a little tricky for you, Streeter," Alphonse said.

"That it could," he replied. "I'm more than open to any better ideas."

Neither Lucci said anything.

12

Freddy Disanto had taught himself to eat slowly for the sole reason that he knew he could fit more in if he did. As a kid, he'd shovel down his mother's food like every meal might be his last. But he'd get full too soon, so he learned to pace himself. He was always big for his age. Big and, since his early teens, hairy. With bones thick as drainpipes, an over-sized skull, and a neck indistinguishable from his shoulders, he could handle a lot of weight without looking fat. He was barrel-chested and had heavy limbs that possessed amazing strength. And it seemed like the D. had dark hair growing everywhere except for maybe on the palms of his hands, the bottom of his feet, and the narrow band of his forehead. Although he was forty-seven, he had looked about the same at twenty-one. Probably would at sixty-five, too. Just sitting there in a wall booth at Pagliacci's, casually taking in the lin-guine and garlic bread with his huge hands, he looked forbidding. Streeter watched the D. for a few minutes before he took a deep breath and walked up to him.

"You mind a little company, Mr. Disanto?" His hands were in his coat side pockets as he stood directly across the booth, looking down at the top of the D.'s head. There was no immediate response, and Streeter could hear the uneven sound of Pagliacci's indoor fountain somewhere behind him. They were in the big room, which was about two-thirds full of people, and still the fountain was loud enough to be heard. The man eating didn't look up directly, but Streeter caught a flash in his direction from his dark eyes and he knew that the D. had spotted him. "I need a few minutes of your time."

Freddy reached to the side, still without looking up, and grabbed another slice of bread. He put it to his mouth and took a surprisingly tiny bite from it. Almost dainty. Then he chewed like he was counting the bites. Streeter shifted his weight from one leg to the other and continued to stare at the top of Freddy's head. His hair was black, with a few white ones salted around the temples. He wore it long but it was thinning a little in front, about like Streeter's. The bounty hunter thought briefly of the minoxidil he'd started using a week or so ago. He was about to make his request again when Freddy finally spoke.

"I'm eating and I don't know you," he said without looking up. "That should answer your question."

Streeter cleared his throat softly. "I just need a few minutes and, besides, we seem to know a lot of the same people."

Freddy's head lifted slightly but he still didn't look up. "Yeah? Like who?" He picked up his glass of red wine and put it to his mouth, lowering his head slightly as he did so.

"Like Al Lucci and Mitch Bosco," he said slowly,

pronouncing every syllable distinctly. "Manny Ramirez." He paused. "Albert Hepp."

That last one brought Freddy's head up till he was looking just above Streeter's belt buckle. Still no eye contact. "Albert? Where do you know him from?"

"Around. I didn't actually know him personally, but I know about him and his poker-playing habits. He and his friends seem to like the game almost as much as you do, and I hear that they figured out a way to win. Big."

This time, the D. carefully set his wineglass down and looked right into Streeter's face. He sized up the man in front of him, in the black leather coat with the white sweatshirt underneath. The guy was about his height, and Freddy could see that the legs packed in the tight blue jeans were nearly as thick as his own. There was a calmness about the man that said he'd be inclined to stand there all day if necessary.

"Ramirez too, huh? You know where he is right about now?" the D. asked.

Streeter shook his head and took a step forward so that his thighs were touching the table. "But I know a few things about that whole situation. In fact, about everything. West Vail, Albert Hepp's demise, your interest in Al Lucci's place."

Freddy sat back and ran his tongue between his top teeth and the inside of his upper lip. It seemed to take him about half an hour to do it. "Yeah?"

"Yeah. You mind if I call you Freddy?"

"Who are you?" The D. ignored his question.

"My name's Streeter."

"What's a Streeter?"

"I work for Alphonse Lucci." He could see a flicker of a frown when Freddy heard that. "In fact, I'm a good friend of his. That's why I'm here. Because I think this whole thing between you and Mr. Lucci is getting way out of hand and it's time we talked it out and got a few things straight." Streeter took his hands out of his jacket and rested them on the table, leaning in slightly as he did. "That would save everyone a lot of trouble and time. Why not hear me out? It won't cost you a penny."

Freddy reached for his wineglass again, still looking directly into Streeter's eyes. "One thing I know for sure, nothing worth a shit is free." His head moved a tad to the left and down, indicating that the man in front of him could sit. "So talk."

Once in the booth, Streeter moved the bread plate away from in front of him. "Here's the deal, Freddy. You want to buy out part of Mr. Lucci's business interests but he really isn't inclined to sell. And ever since he informed you of his reluctance, you've been letting people know how unhappy you are about it." Streeter waited for a moment, but the D. didn't respond. "Not only that, but lately some very weird things have been happening around Mr. Lucci. There was a fire next to his place in West Vail. Right next door, in fact. Then one of his friendly little card games got taken off earlier this week."

"This is supposed to be new information?" Freddy picked at his linguine without looking at Streeter. "I was at the fucking game myself."

"So I'm told." Streeter shot him a grin. "I heard you got pushed around some."

The D. stopped chewing his food for a second or two but said nothing.

"Anyhow, here's the new part," Streeter continued. "First off, Mr. Lucci has hired me to keep an eye on him and to make sure no more weird things happen. And I take my job so seriously you wouldn't believe it. Also, I have a lot of friends on the Denver Police Department and we chat from time to time. What I told them today is that there was a problem at Mr. Lucci's place on Monday and that a couple of days later one of the guys who helped cause that problem ended up dead in Wyoming. I also showed them a fax that Mr. Lucci got right after that death. From you, no less." He paused to let it sink in. "They were very interested in that. Then I told them that someone saw a certain Mitch Bosco leave the scene of that West Vail fire last week and that Mr. Bosco works for you periodically. This really got their interest. Finally, I told them about Mr. Lucci refusing to sell you his property and how unpleasant you got over that. Almost threatening. By that time, you might say that my friends were all ears."

Streeter leaned back in his seat and watched the D. for a moment. He felt loose and decided to ad-lib a little. Frank had taught him years ago to divide and conquer, so he thought he'd give that a shot. "They were so intrigued that they said they'd do a little looking into the situation. But here's the funny part. They said that Mitch Bosco had already been in touch with them about some legal problems he has and that he seemed inclined to cooperate with them on other matters if it would help keep his sorry butt out of jail. They said that your name was mentioned in that context."

Freddy turned to Streeter now. "Is that right? You get around."

"That I do." Streeter nodded. "And I want you to know that I'm going to stay around. Around Mr. Lucci and his family, specifically. I'm going to be watching them like crazy from now on. My impression from my friends at the DPD is that they might be doing the same. And one more thing, Freddy. Mr. Lucci wanted me to let you know that he's been giving your offer on the restaurant a lot of thought."

"And?" His voice was more bored than ever.

"And he's decided for dead solid certain that he won't sell the place, not even for ten times what you offered. He'll never sell."

Freddy nodded and then looked back to his lunch. "You know, I'm not the brightest guy on earth, so most of what you're saying is going way the hell over my head. I'm not even sure what I have to do with all that stuff. Faxes and fires and whatnot. But if you're saying Lucci doesn't want to sell, that's a surprise to me. 'Cause my impression is that he might be open to more negotiations." He took another small bite from his bread and chewed thoughtfully. "We done here or what?"

"I guess we are. Except that I wouldn't hold my breath waiting for Mr. Lucci to reimburse you for Monday night's theft. It's not gonna happen. Not ever." Streeter slid out of the booth. After looking back down at Freddy for a moment, he walked toward the door without saying another word.

The D. stared at him until he was gone and then he grabbed a tiny cell phone from inside his sport coat, punched in Mitch's number. "Yeah, it's me. We gotta get together soon. Yeah, tomorrow night'll be good. I got more work for you."

13

It was said of Karen Maples when she was a prosecutor in Pittsburgh that if she hadn't gone into law she would have made one outstanding dominatrix. You always half expected her to pull a whip and a ball gag from her briefcase. Rarin' Karen, as they called her, was all of five feet five inches, but she had the audacity of a rhino in mating season. Determined and always focused. What Karen wanted, Karen got. Plain to see that from a mile away. How she carried herself, her shoulders set high, searing Joan Crawford stare, drawing in deep breaths that made her breasts rise with authority. Seemed to take her forever to exhale. Walked like she couldn't get around fast enough and talked in short, don't-screw-with-me bursts. Her demeanor demanded attention and, having graduated second in her class from the University of Texas Law School, this woman could back it up. One solid glare from her could suck the oxygen from a small room.

Watching her now on the phone at her desk, Todd Janek could feel himself getting as stiff as rolled steel. He was totally infatuated with the woman. Not a terrific idea, considering he worked for her. She wasn't particularly attractive. Decent-looking enough, but nothing special. Karen had a pale complexion offset by thick hair the color of fresh tar. Small hazel eyes that looked innocent and set up an opponent nicely. Her chin was a little small and weak, but she did have a great smile. Slightly chunky legs that flowed down from a slightly chunky waist. But Todd's interest in her was spurred more by her aggressive style than by her looks. He found her attitude to be irresistible.

"You're talking nothing but utter nonsense here, Clarence," she was saying into the receiver. "Your guy takes a woman to a hotel out on East Colfax, plies her with coke and brandy, they have sex—which she swears was clearly *not* consensual—and he goes out to his car and gets a sawed-off shotgun. Then he brings it back to the room and passes out. When he wakes up, half his face is pushed in and she's holding the gun. Your guy"—she glanced down at the file in front of her and read—"Tyrone Moore, got a few stitches out of the deal. He's lucky that's all he got. If he'd had shells in that thing he'd be dead now and you'd be representing Miss Franklin on at least a manslaughter charge.

"So Tyrone's looking at—what?—kidnapping, sex assault, possession with intent to deliver, and possession of a lethal weapon by a convicted felon. I assume you're aware that Tyrone has a fairly colorful felony record." She looked at the file quickly again. "Hell, he'd only been out of prison a grand total of three weeks when this happened." She paused and cleared her throat. "I can prove all of it and you want me to drop everything but the drug charge. What kind of drugs would I have to be on to even consider that?"

She looked straight ahead—past Todd, sitting across from

her, like he wasn't there. Her features were drawn in a tight frown. Todd really liked her war face. As she listened to Clarence on the other end, Karen rocked slightly in her chair.

"Who gives a flying you-know-what if the gun wasn't loaded?" she asked as she suddenly stopped rocking. "His just having the damned thing is enough to meet the statute requirements. That alone gets Mr. Moore eight to twelve. And also, who cares if Miss Franklin has a couple of prostitution convictions? The last one was months ago. She's obviously left the life and this is the thanks she gets. Drugged and raped. I can't wait to hear you tell a jury that a tiny little thing like Miss Franklin beat up a man as large as your Tyrone. Give me a break. He could play for the Broncos if he wasn't in prison most of the time."

She paused again, listening hard. "No, Clarence, *you're* fucked all the way around on this one. Not me. I've got nothing better to do than go slam-dunk you and your client in court. I look forward to it. I really do. You go tell Tyrone to get ready to head back down to Canon City. I'll see if I can get him roomed up with one of those maniacs from the Aryan Brotherhood." She paused again and lowered her voice. "Yes, yes. There might be some wiggle room on that kidnapping-and-assault business. But the rest of it's there for good. You better just prepare your guy for the hammer coming down." She listened for a moment. "That's good, Clarence. Go talk to my boss. I'm sure he's in today. Do you want me to transfer you over?" Another pause. "Not right now, huh? You do that, Clarence. You get back to me on it."

When Karen hung up, she kept looking straight ahead for a moment and then she focused on Todd Janek. "Why do they stick me with these turkeys now? As if I don't have enough to think about. But, no, I have to fart around with this." She threw her hand out toward the file on her desk.

"I've got a hooker robbing a scumbag and then beating the poor slob half to death with his own gun after he passes out. Hell, the coke was even hers. The best we've got is that possession-of-deadly-weapon rap, and the lab isn't even sure if the thing was operational. Lucky for me Clarence wants to go to trial less than I do. I'll let him and Tyrone stew with it for a week or so, and then we'll deal out. No way I'm going to put this mess in front of a jury. I tell you, Todd, I'm batting a thousand percent in Denver District Court and I intend to keep my record that way."

Todd felt himself getting even more aroused. Karen was about his age—thirty-four, give or take. But she acted like she'd been dealing with defense lawyers for fifty years. The perfect trial advocate, Karen Maples had it all. She was smart, aggressive, combative, and would rather die of a brain tumor than admit she was wrong or in trouble. Losing was out of the question.

Finally, Karen squinted at him in deep concentration. She liked Todd, the DA's investigator assigned to her. Pleasant-looking, thin and blond with a pale, narrow mustache. They'd worked together on a few cases and he was no fool. Plus, he treated her with deference bordering on affection. That didn't happen to her often. Especially the affection part.

"What was it you wanted to see me about?" she asked. "I hope it's not bad news. This thing with Bosco and Kostas is coming together in—what?—less than two weeks to go. I sure don't need any bad news, Todd."

He frowned briefly and then cleared his throat. "Well, there is one small item you might want to know about. The guys down in Vice are pretty pissed about Mitch Bosco. Apparently, he's been moving a little product lately and he's not even trying to be cool about it. Vice could have nailed him last week and they don't get why we're holding them back. I blew some smoke at them yesterday, but they're still not happy." He shrugged. "I don't think we should be, either. Bosco's giving us Kostas but he's getting a free ride on that gun-sale thing. Not a bad deal. You should try and rein him."

Karen sat up, frowning. "You're right about that. Nailing Ted Kostas'll be nice, but it's not like I can build a career around it. Still, I'm not going to allow some little chicken-shit dime-bag pot arrest to stand in the way of this sting."

"Coke, not pot." Todd shifted in his chair. "Bosco's moving coke."

"Whatever. You get my meaning."

"Look, Karen," he said, "I know how bringing Kostas down would be nice, and how we need Bosco to do that. But he's being a total jerk lately. We can't lose control of the guy."

"You're right. Also, let's see if we can move things up. Work on getting me those cars a little sooner, Todd." Karen leaned forward in her chair. "This should be a fairly simple matter. Bosco hooks our guys up with Kostas and they sell him the hot cars. Ba-da-*bing*. We all go home happy except for Kostas, who goes to jail." She paused. "The more I think about this sting, the less enthused I get. I know Ted Kostas used to run a decent-sized operation, but he's by himself now. Strictly small potatoes and dumb as a post. Let's make it quick and painless."

Todd nodded. "I'll see what I can do about the cars. That shouldn't be much of a problem. They're just loaners." In terms of ambition, Todd was a comer all the way, and he liked working with Karen. "I'm with you one hundred percent on this, and I'll deal with the Vice people. But try and keep Bosco in line."

She nodded and gave him a smile. "I hate talking to that

fool. Mr. Success. You should hear him. Always quoting this self-help junk. But I'll give him a call. Anything else?"

"Actually, yes." Todd stood up and looked down at her, taking a deep breath. "I'm wondering if we could have dinner together sometime soon. Tonight would work for me."

Karen's headed bobbed slightly while she considered his proposal. She took him in with one hard glance. She had already been through a messy office romance back in Pittsburgh. But even Karen did not live by work alone, and Todd did have a trim build and nice blue eyes. Plenty of beach-boy hair, too. And he was a worker. No doubt about that.

"But not for me," she said slowly. Then she added, "Tomorrow night should. We can catch up on the case while we're eating."

"Great," he said. Yeah, right, he thought. Dinner on a Friday night after work. Dinner and drinks. We'll just do that catching-up thing.

14

Ted Kostas walked from his car with the 387 serial-number stickers he'd spent the day scraping off of that many stolen color-television sets jammed into his various pants and shirt pockets. He thought it might be a prudent idea to get rid of them fairly quickly. Ted figured the most he could handle would be explaining why he had all those hot sets sitting the garage at his place. "Holy shit, officer," he could say. "You tell me those things were lifted from a railroad car the other night? I think I read something about that in the papers. Believe me, I had no idea when my friend asked me to store the stupid things that they were the exact same Sonys that I'd been reading about. No way in hell I would have done it if I knew they were stolen. Like how could I know that?"

But explaining how the serial-number tags ended up in his pockets was another matter entirely, and Ted well knew it. He walked to the middle of the darkened alley behind some stores on 38th Street, near Federal Boulevard. The alley was randomly chosen by him as he drove around the West Side, quite a distance from his place. On one side of him were the backs of stores, on the other were garages for the houses that fronted on 39th Street. Ted was carrying a large tin of lighter fluid and his ancient Zippo. He figured he'd burn the whole batch of stickers and be done with it. No one knew him around there. Glancing up and down the alley and then at the backs of the houses, he didn't see anyone. He knelt between a big blue Dumpster and the side of a wooden garage and set the metal Zippo and the fluid on the ground. Fifty-seven years old, and carrying an extra forty-odd pounds around, he found kneeling no small task. First he stroked his gray beard a couple of times, then he started emptying his pockets alongside the lighter and fluid. Within a minute or so he had piled all of the sticky-backed serial tags neatly about two feet from the garage.

Ted stood up, one knee cracking loudly. Getting old is hell, he thought. Glancing around one more time, he still saw no one. Not at this time of night. It had to be after ten. A working-class Mexican neighborhood like this, he didn't expect to see anyone out and about. So he knelt again, grabbed the tin, and started squeezing the fluid onto the pile in front of him. As the tin got about half empty, Ted heard a car coming down the alley behind him. Slowly, he half turned in that direction while still draining the tin. As his head turned, his arm with the fluid moved up, too, sending a thick spray of the stuff along the ground and onto the side of the garage. Ted, not being what anyone would describe as an astute man, didn't notice this as he listened to the approaching vehicle. Before the car got anywhere near where he was squatting, it stopped and backed out of the alley.

The stolen-television fence then turned back to the job at hand and finished dumping the fluid. He dropped the tin onto the pile, picked up the old Zippo, and clicked it open. As an afterthought, he pulled a Camel nonfilter from the pack in his shirt pocket and put it between his lips. First he lit the cigarette and then he moved the lighter over the pile. The fluid caught like crazy right off, making a harsh popping sound and sending flames almost a foot straight up, so they almost caught Ted's beard. The Greek, as he was sometimes known, shot his head back to avoid the flames and quickly stood up. Quickly for him, anyhow.

"The hell?" he muttered as he watched the flames move with amazing speed from the pile over the trail of fluid he'd squirted on the ground, which was covered with dry, dead leaves. From there, the fire silently moved a few feet up the dry-rotted wall of the old garage.

Ted stood there and took it all in for a moment before moving around the burning pile and stepping to the garage side, which was going up rather nicely by now. A swath of about two square feet was in flames. With the cigarette still in his mouth, Ted swiped at the wall once with his right hand. He obviously had no formal training in this type of thing. His hand smacked hard against the wood, and immediately he could feel the sting of a burn.

"Aggggh," he yelled and bounced back a step.

His eyes were wide and he looked around for a moment. Then he stomped once at the flames on the ground with his left foot. The bottom of his shoe lingered on the leaves longer than he had intended. Several of the parched leaves clung to it as he finally lifted his foot. Now he was standing there with the garage going up next to him and his one foot raised about eighteen inches off the ground, also on fire.

"Muthafucka," he yelped, hopping back away from the garage and then stamping his shoe down several times until the flames went out. He looked at the smoldering shoe for a few bewildered seconds, turned around, and headed back to his car, figuring who gives a rip about some old run-down garage. Certainly not Ted Kostas. By the time he made it to the big Volvo and got inside, the flames were moving slightly farther up the garage wall. The inside of his car quickly smelled like burned rubber from his shoe.

Driving to the end of the alley, Ted shot a glance in his rearview mirror. He could see that a fair chunk of the garage wall was engulfed, which didn't bother him much, for he assumed that meant that the serial-number stickers were history by now. Ted figured he'd done what he'd set out to do, so he was feeling okay about himself by the time he wheeled out of the alley. Still, he silently cursed the fact that he had to be out at that time of night getting rid of the stickers. If he'd had a crew to help him he could have just passed the work on to one of them. Maybe they could figure out a way to do the job right. Even a partner would be nice. But he never could find anyone who'd work with him. At least not for any extended period of time. Long ago, Ted had resigned himself to the life of a lonely fence and petty thief. At least it beat working for a living. Probably. And he could move the merchandise when it was available. Made more than decent money most times.

Then he flashed on the cars he would be getting soon. A couple of new Jaguars, no less. At least if that clown Mitch Bosco came through like he said. This would be the move that would give Kostas some real breathing room. He figured his end would be pushing around the forty-thousand-dollar range. Maybe more. With that nice little thought close to him, he headed back south, to his side of town and a refrigerator full of beer.

15

Shortly after ten that Friday morning, Streeter walked out to his old brown Buick, which was parked in front of the church, and headed to Denver's midtown Capitol Hill section and Mitch Bosco's place. Fortunately, Mitch's driver's license had been renewed on his birthday, a scant three months earlier. Renewed with a current address. That surprised the bounty hunter, because people who lived outside the law rarely did things like keep their licenses current or register to vote. But here was Mitch trotting down to DMV as he turned forty-two, dutifully giving them his correct address.

As he drove south on Broadway, Streeter thought of his conversation the day before with Freddy the D. If any good had come from it, he couldn't see it. The man sat there impassive as a corpse, eating ever so slowly, reacting to nothing. Letting on that he thought Alphonse's restaurant was still in play, which was not good news. This thing was a

long way from over, Streeter thought as he moved east onto
Colfax Avenue. But what did he expect? That the D. would
fold up because Streeter had worn a leather jacket and talked
a little tough? Damn, that Disanto was one big man. Bigger
than the bounty hunter himself. A head like a concrete gar-
goyle, too.

On Wednesday night, Streeter and Frank had argued
about his talking to the D. at all. Frank, the lawman even in
retirement, had insisted that Alphonse, Sheri, and Streeter
trot down to the police station and lay it all out for the
detectives. Streeter had explained why that wouldn't work.
Not with Sheri and her father both refusing to say a word
about the card-game robbery or seeing Bosco in West Vail.
And the fax didn't tie Disanto to anything, either. Even
Frank had to admit that when he studied it. Way too vague.
Earlier on Wednesday, Streeter had tried to interest Detective Carey in Disanto, but what little he could hint at didn't
even raise an eyebrow.

Now it was time for the second phase of his plan. Tail
Mitch and let him know it. If he couldn't rattle Freddy,
maybe he could rattle Bosco. Streeter knew it would be easy
for him to let Mitch know he was there. One-man, moving
surveillances were difficult. Stay close, chances are he'll see
you. Hang back, you'll probably lose him. Streeter didn't
have time to follow the man for long and still keep an eye on
the Luccis, so he decided to be obvious.

Mitch lit a Salem 100 and thought of his conversation
with Freddy the D. the day before. Freddy had sounded
madder than usual and left no doubt he wanted to turn up
the heat on Lucci. Fine with Mitch. "Opportunities are for
those who are open," he'd memorized. "Seize them quickly."
He needed the money. Mitch had himself on a savings plan
that gave him a projected retirement date of 2011. He'd turn
fifty-three that year, and at his current rate of savings, what

with Disanto's jobs, the odd coke deal, other moves he'd get from time to time, and tax-sheltered investments, Mitch figured to have just over eight hundred thousand socked away by then. Enough to retire in close to style. Since he'd begun fashioning his "Ladder of Success," Mitch had watched his money closely. Although he lived in a decent high-rise apartment building four blocks south of the State Capitol, his rent included heat, utilities, and furniture. "Stay mobile and don't tie up income," he'd heard on an investment tape. "A penny saved is two pennies earned." So Mitch was anxious to get back at it with Lucci. That meant money, plus showing the D. that he wasn't a total screwup after West Vail.

He scratched at his chest under the silk bathrobe he wore, thinking about what the D. had told him on Thursday. Who was this bounty hunter Disanto was talking about? Some big, cocky dude who mentioned the cops repeatedly to the D. He didn't go into any details, but Freddy said that this Streeter guy specifically talked about Mitch. Not fatal, but definitely not good, either.

"Guy seems to be no stranger to you," the D. had told him on the phone. Then there was that long, dramatic pause, like he wanted Mitch to confess something. "No stranger at all," Disanto had concluded.

Bosco shrugged. Whatever the hell that meant. Not much he could do about it this morning. He figured he'd learn more that night, when they hooked up to discuss the new job. For now, he'd take a quick shower and then head over to talk to Ted Kostas. Iron out a few details on the Jaguar buy. Be good to get that monkey off his back, Mitch thought as he headed down the hall to the bathroom. Let Kostas do the time Mitch should be getting for selling a couple of pieces to an undercover cop. Bargains and shortcuts. That's how the criminal-justice system worked. Nobody knew that better than him. Giving up Kostas was just part of the cost of doing business.

Streeter parked almost directly in front of Mitch's building. He opened the glove compartment and pulled out the paperwork Ronnie'd gotten at DMV. On her own initiative, she'd also gotten automobile-registration information on all the vehicles Disanto and Bosco owned. Streeter glanced at the plate number for Bosco's 1986 green Volvo station wagon. Making a mental note of the number, he got out of his car. He looked up and down Pearl Street, straining to find Bosco's car. After walking south a bit, he noticed a parking lot on that side of Mitch's building. There it was, the green Volvo wagon. Streeter returned to his car and backed up slightly so he could watch both the front door of the high-rise and the lot.

Sitting there in his car seat, he thought about old Lucci's problems. Streeter wondered if he could talk Alphonse into the quite sensible option of selling his prime restaurant. Doubtful. Why should he have any luck if Sheri couldn't do it? Then he wondered how far Disanto would go to get the place. Can't get much heavier than arson, and if Disanto had killed the guy in Wyoming, well, he was able to do anything. Streeter struggled to dismiss the thought. No point in worrying, especially on a stakeout. Frank had told him long ago that you'd drive yourself crazy doing that. Streeter had sat there for forty-five minutes when he saw a man come out the front door. From the way Sheri had described Mitch, he figured this must be his boy. He watched the guy walk slowly to the side parking lot and go to the Volvo station wagon. Mitch, all right.

Bosco took his time unlocking the door and letting the engine warm up once he got inside. He didn't look around much, but lit a cigarette and finally put the car in reverse.

When he got to the curb, Streeter quickly started his Buick and put it into gear. Mitch glanced his way without seeming to notice the old brown car starting up just across from him. Then he turned right on Pearl. Streeter followed him at just over a car length as he drove to Broadway and then south, beyond the Valley Highway. Then took a right followed by a left as he curled around for a few more blocks. Streeter stayed so close he figured that only if Mitch were a complete idiot would he not notice him, especially on those empty side roads.

Mitch quickly drove the last few blocks to Ted Kostas's scrap yard. He barely glanced in the rearview mirror the whole time, from what Streeter could see. When he parked in front of the scrap yard, Mitch got out without looking around. The bounty hunter stopped about a half-block behind the Volvo and kept his engine running. Mitch walked to a small gate next to the large gate in front of the driveway leading into the yard. He opened it and went inside, closing it carefully behind him. Then he headed up the drive and went into a tiny building.

After sitting there for a minute or so, Streeter finally shut off his engine. He got out and moved slowly toward the yard. An ancient, rusty metal sign marked "T.K. Scrap" hung slightly lopsided on the fence near the entrance. Actually, the place was too small to be a junkyard. It was more of a large auto-repair lot. A brick building was on the left, a side yard containing maybe a dozen gutted cars on the right. A short driveway between the two led up to a grimy shack that looked like it once was a small gas station. That was where Mitch had gone. Next to the shack was a narrow pen housing two angry-looking Dobermans. Streeter walked past the place and then turned around and walked slowly back. If Bosco hadn't noticed him until now, this would probably get his attention.

When Mitch got inside the shack, he went right to the tiny office in the rear. Ted Kostas was working on a sub sandwich, sitting at a desk that was cramped with smudged papers and car parts.

"You here already?" Kostas asked as Mitch entered the room. He held a can of Coke in one hand and waved the other in greeting.

"No, I'll be coming in an hour or so," Mitch shot back. He gave his eyes a what-the-hell roll as he stood in front of the desk. "Someone followed me all the way from my place."

Kostas frowned deeply and set down his Coke. "Cops?"

"I doubt it. He was so close on my ass, it had to a been a civilian." Mitch paused, thinking about the bounty hunter that Disanto had mentioned. He jerked his head toward the front of the shack. "Let's see if he's still out there."

Kostas got up from his chair and followed Mitch to the small window facing the street. They stopped a couple of steps back from it, both men squinting to see outside. About a minute later, a big man in washed-out jeans and a gray sweater strolled past the driveway entrance, turning his head several times to look into the lot. Must be the bounty hunter, Mitch decided.

"That the guy?" Kostas asked, still staring out the window.

"Yeah. That's no cop."

Ted turned to Mitch, his frown deepening. "Better not be. You bring heat down on me now, that deal we got is off."

Mitch glanced at him. A string of what looked like roast beef hung off the bottom of his beard. "Don't soil your pants up. I saw the guy all the way. Remember, 'It's better to observe than to be observed.'"

"You can cut that baloney right now," Ted said, sounding mildly pissed. "From where I'm standing, it looks like you were *observed* pretty good."

"Calm down. This has nothing to do with you. This guy, I've been warned about him. I thought he might be a little sharper, but it's okay he's none too bright." Mitch bit his lower lip in thought. Finally, he asked, "You got a piece in here?"

Ted shrugged. "A small .22 in my desk. Why?"

"Your car out in the back alley?"

Ted nodded.

"Go get the keys. It's about time I teach this dipshit a lesson. Give me the keys to your car and the .22."

"Why?" Kostas took a couple of steps back from the window. "I thought we were supposed to discuss that Jaguar deal. You know I don't like talking on the phone about that."

"Just give me the car and the piece. I want to get this guy off my butt. I'll come back later, when the dust settles."

"What dust?"

"The dust from me firing off your gun, is what dust. Don't worry. This guy's not likely to call the police, and like I said, this has nothing to do with you."

Kostas ran one hand over his beard. When he got to the chunk of meat he pulled it out and away from his face, studying it closely. Then he stuck it in his mouth and chewed. "Okay. Just so it's like you say."

"Relax. I have one more meeting with these people with the discount cars and then they bring them down here. You give them the money and it's over. Except for you selling them on your end."

"That's all covered. Just so I know I can trust these people you found."

Mitch nodded. "They're solid." He paused for a moment and held out his hand. "The keys and the piece."

Kostas went to his desk and took a small revolver out of

the top drawer. Then he dug into his pockets and pulled out his key ring. Handing both to Mitch, he asked, "How long you gonna need my car?"

"An hour or so, maybe. Don't worry. We'll talk when I get back." Mitch put the gun in his pants pocket and studied the keys, frowning.

"It's the Volvo keys," Ted offered. "Like yours but not a wagon. White one, right out back."

Mitch nodded. "When I leave, you go out in the yard and act like you got a life. Act busy and curious so the guy moves on."

"For how long?"

"Till you hear a signal from me. You'll know it. Then you can come back and finish your lunch."

As Streeter slowed down in front of the gate, a man suddenly walked out of the shack. He was wearing filthy green work overalls and steel-tipped safety boots, and he looked from side to side as he moved toward the other building. His round, inexpressive face hid behind a thick gray beard. Streeter pegged him to be about sixty. Before he got to the building, the guy stopped and shot him a glance. At that, Streeter picked up the pace back toward his Buick.

Mitch shoved the Volvo into drive and headed quickly down the alley. When he'd gone about two hundred feet, he stopped behind a long toolshed. He rammed the car into park and, leaving the engine running, got out. Pulling the small gun from his pocket, he checked to make sure it was loaded. Then he walked along the side of the shed toward the street. When he got just about to the front corner, he could see the man approaching his Buick, which was parked out front. Mitch half squatted with the shed on his right, and a small evergreen shielding him partially on his left. The man who had followed him stopped, glanced back toward T.K. Scrap, and then moved the final few feet to his car. He got into it and sat behind the wheel.

Streeter looked through his windshield and decided he'd gotten his message through to Mitch, who'd probably sent the old man into the yard to check him out. Enough of this game. Maybe he'd follow Mitch the next day as a reminder. He reached down and pushed the key forward, and the Buick turned over. Next he heard an explosion off to his right and behind him. Several chunks of glass from his rear passenger's door hit the back of his head and he could feel them cutting into his skin. Automatically, he moved down to protect himself. Then he heard two more explosions from the same direction and more glass shattered around him. The inside of the car smelled like burned metal.

Following the third shot, Mitch put the revolver down by his side and watched the Buick for a moment. The second and third shots had gone in through the front passenger's window and out the driver's window. Close enough to give the bounty hunter a good earache, Mitch reasoned. As he started to back off, he could see that the driver's head was still low, only the top of it visible. He turned and trotted back to the idling Volvo. He was in it and all the way to the end of the alley before Streeter dared to lift his head up again.

The bounty hunter squinted around the car and realized how close he'd come to being hit. He wondered if it was a warning or bad shooting. Then he looked back toward the scrap yard in time to see the old man turning and walking toward the shack. Obviously, the bullets hadn't come from him. Streeter shook off his shock and put the Buick into reverse. He backed up, looking alternately to both sides of the street. By the time he got to the end of the block, he realized that whoever had done it was gone. He put the car in drive, but kept his foot on the brake. Reaching into his glove box, he pulled out a cell phone and debated for a few seconds whether to call the police. Instead, he threw it on the seat next to him and touched the back of his head with his left hand, feeling what must be blood starting to mat his hair down. Then he headed north, back to the church.

Once inside the shack, Ted Kostas moved silently to his desk and sat down. Damned Bosco sure didn't like people following him, he thought. He picked up the sub sandwich and studied it. Then he took a huge bite and started to chew. Like Mitch said, this had nothing to do with him.

16

"I'd say, Mitchie, that it's time for us to put her into a higher gear with the old man," Freddy said.

He and Mitch were sitting on the steps of Denver's Civic Center, an amphitheater in a park between City Hall and the State Capitol. It was cool that Friday evening, the upper forties at most, and getting dark, but Freddy seemed comfortable in just a Banlon shirt and pleated slacks. For his part, Mitch was pulling on a fresh Salem 100, shivering from time to time in the raw night air, and wishing that Disanto would get to the point. Freddy was trying to act calm, but he was clearly furious: his jaw kept clenching and his eyes looked glazed.

"That business with the Ramirez Boys the other night . . ." Freddy paused and studied Mitch. "That was the Cheese Man's doing all the way. I know that for a fact."

"Yeah?" Mitch's eyes narrowed. "How you know that?"

Freddy nodded solemnly. "Just trust me. I know."

Right, Mitch thought. You know everything. "Why would Lucci set up his own game? Makes no sense."

"At first, that was my thought, too." The D. shifted his weight on the cold concrete. "But he must be so pissed at me about Vail that he thought it was worth it. Who knows how an old guy like that thinks? He's pretty confused these days." Freddy looked off for a moment before he went on. "The point is, I gotta get some real fear working in him. I've been talking to my associates in Arizona and they want this deal settled in the next week or so. Lucci sells to me fast or the Arizona people say they'll drop the whole project." He shrugged. "Me included. They'll sell what we got for a tax write-off and move on to something else. Without me. I put way too much time and effort and dough into this thing to let that happen. You follow me, Mitchie?"

Mitch frowned and considered the question. He also considered the pressure Freddy was getting from Arizona. Bosco knew all about that, but he was still surprised to see how it shook the D. He debated whether to tell Freddy about his run-in with the bounty hunter that morning and decided against it. "You asking me to whack the old man or what?" he finally asked.

Freddy shook his head. "You do that, how'm I supposed to negotiate with a dead man? Believe me, the thought of taking him out makes me very happy. Especially with that crap from the card game. Those guys roughin' me up. But I need him alive if I'm going to buy his place."

"I'm just asking, is all." Mitch stomped out his cigarette. "Why don't you tell me what it is you want?"

"I'll do that." Freddy stood up and looked down at Mitch. "The old man has a car he keeps under wraps. We're talking about a 1979 Lincoln Town Car here. Lucci loves the thing. What I'm saying is that we do a little number on that car so it causes the old man problems."

Mitch studied the D. "I gather that when you say 'we' you mean me."

"You got that right. I'll pay you like always. Not to mention that the last time we spoke you said something about making up for that bungled job in Vail."

"Not to mention, huh?"

Freddy shot him a hard stare. "Not to mention. This is how it'll go down. Lucci keeps the Lincoln parked in a garage about four doors down from his house. He has a one-car garage, so he rents another one from a neighbor. Like I said, the old man's totally nuts about that car. He only drives it on special occasions, like to Mass every Sunday morning. And he's the only guy who drives the thing. No one touches that Lincoln besides him. That means, Mitchie, that if someone were to fuck up the car, like, say, bleed the brakes dry or whatever, Alphonse Lucci would be sure to get the fallout."

Slowly, the seated man lifted his head to make eye contact with Disanto. He nodded, but said nothing.

"I checked out the garage," Freddy continued, "and getting inside should be a piece of cake. No security system, no outer lighting, and just one flimsy lock. You should be in and out of there in no time." He looked deeply into Mitch's eyes. "My suggestion is that you do it early tomorrow morning. Lucci probably won't drive it during the day tomorrow, but first thing Sunday morning he will."

Mitch sat there, looking up. His body swayed slightly in the darkness. "Any chance he goes to church by himself?"

"I don't see what that matters to you."

Mitch pulled another cigarette from his pack and thought of how, if Alphonse drove the Lincoln and banged it up, old lady Lucci would probably get hurt, too. He remained silent.

"All you gotta worry about is doing the job right," Freddy was now saying. "Bleed the brakes. The old man won't get far before he runs into something. It shouldn't kill him, but it will screw his precious car, and I'll make sure he gets the point from my end. You okay with all this?"

"I suppose."

"Outstanding." The D. pulled a slip of paper from his pants pocket. "Here's the old man's address and the location of the garage."

Mitch stood up, taking the paper from Freddy. Then he nodded and started toward where he'd parked his car.

"Not so fast, Mitchie."

He stopped and faced Freddy again. "What?"

"We're driving past the house and the garage right now. You and me. I wanna make sure that you know exactly where to go later. We don't need any of the Cheese Man's neighbors getting their brakes screwed up by mistake, do we?"

Compared with Ben Champine, Space Lucci seemed nearly functional. Although only three months younger than Space, Ben was functionally illiterate and had served nearly four of his twenty-one years locked up for various controlled-substance violations. His drug of choice was primarily anything he could get his hands on. Pot, speed, hallucinogens, crack, airplane glue, meth, cough medicine, alcohol. If it was placed in front of young Ben, he consumed it, somehow. The two of them were sitting in the huge guest bedroom at Alphonse Lucci's house that Saturday night, smoking a third joint and drinking the old man's bourbon. Alphonse and Maria had just left to visit her sister and would be gone for at least three hours. Ben and Space had come to the house earlier for lasagna and were planning on spending the night. Space did that often on Saturday nights, and Ben, well, he didn't much care where he was as long as he could get high for free, which is what Space had promised him. Not to mention that this was a special night. Ben's twenty-first birthday. He kept forgetting that, but Space now reminded him as they toasted each other with a stiff drink and a toke from the yellow plastic bong.

"I'm thinking, like, we should do something different tonight, man," Ben said as he passed the pipe to his friend.

Space frowned in confusion and said nothing.

"Like maybe tool on downtown and get some women," Ben continued, nodding at the reasonableness of his plan.

"Cool." Neither of them said anything for a long time as they both continued to work on the bong and their drinks. Finally, Space spoke up. "Let's go, man."

They stood and began to move toward the steps leading down to the first floor. But when they got to the top of the stairs, they stopped and faced each other.

"Hell, man," Ben said. "How we gonna do it? No ride."

Space's eyes narrowed in recognition of the fact that they had hitchhiked to his grandfather's house. Not only did neither man own a car, but only Space had ever actually gotten a driver's license, and that had been revoked over a year ago. Ben had quit trying for his after a bad accident on his third test. Also, Ben had to consider that he had never been with a woman in the carnal sense of the word. Between drugs and lockup, he had never gotten around to actually losing his virginity.

"It doesn't matter," Space said. "We don't know any women, anyhow. I'm like thinkin' that we should stay here and just chill some more."

Ben frowned at the thought. "Not tonight, man. My birthday."

Space pulled his head back and smiled. "Right."

"Doesn't your grandpa have a car?"

"Sure. A Ford Escort. But that's what they took."

"Too bad, man. I guess we do stay here and chill."

But neither of them moved. Suddenly, Space smiled

again. From somewhere in the back of his mind, he recalled the Cheese Man's Lincoln. "Wait, man. He's got another ride. This old blue car he keeps down the block. He drove me to court in it one time. The keys must be around here somewhere."

"Excellent. Let's go."

It took them nearly half an hour to find the keys, which turned out to be hanging on the hooks near the back kitchen door where Alphonse and Maria kept objects like umbrellas and keys. Of all things. Then they walked the four houses down to the garage, and it took them several more minutes to wrestle the correct key into the side door. Once inside, Space opened the overhead while Ben hopped in behind the wheel. On the way over, they'd decided that the birthday boy should drive. Ben fumbled with the keys as Space jumped into the passenger's seat. With only a little illumination coming in from the streetlight, it was dark in the car.

"This thing's huge. Like something out of *Star Wars*," Ben said as he put the key in the ignition. He turned over the engine, which was loud enough all by itself. But when he tromped the accelerator it sounded like they were cranking up a rocket ship in a closet. "Excellent!" Ben, smiling broadly, hollered over the roar. "No problem getting women with this baby," he added. Looking out past the steering wheel and through the windshield, he realized that he could barely focus his eyes. In passing, he wondered if that would cause him any problems driving.

"Let's do it," Space yelled back.

Ben, his mouth open wide in concentration, nodded once and then dropped the car into reverse. He tromped the gas pedal again with his right foot, and before he could turn his head completely to look out the back window in the direction they were headed, the old Lincoln squealed out of the tiny garage.

Both boys yelped in confusion as the giant car rumbled over the driveway. They had gone almost to the end of the thirty-foot drive when Ben collected himself enough to pull his foot off the gas and ram it onto the brakes. He shoved down hard, instantly ramming the pedal all the way to the floorboards. He tried to yell out to Space, but his mouth worked about as well as the brakes. Nothing came out as the car flew the few remaining few feet of driveway and out onto the street.

"Car!" was the best Space could get out as he stared in shock at the parked yellow Honda Prelude sitting perpendicular to the Lincoln immediately across the narrow road. Within seconds, the Town Car shot to the other side of the street, its wide rear end hitting the Prelude at a nearly perfect ninety-degree angle. The right side of the smaller import caved in like it was made of papier-mâché, sending out a loud groan of crushed sheet metal and broken glass.

Ben and Space were shoved hard against the soft bench-seat back when they first hit the Honda. The force of the impact then flung their bodies simultaneously forward; Ben's left temple smashed into the steering wheel, and Space hit the dashboard with the right side of his head an instant later.

When they finally stopped, Space's body shook in pain and bewilderment. He tried to comprehend what had just happened. Cool, he thought finally as he sat there, and wondered how Ben had done that.

17

When he first got to the garage that Saturday night and saw the damage to the rear end of his prized Town Car, Alphonse looked utterly defeated. But the longer he stared at the car, the more furious he became. He was pale, almost bloodless. Once he finally calmed down, he talked to the owner of the Prelude. Got the guy to take a personal check for two thousand dollars toward fixing the side of his car. That and a promise to come to Al personally if it cost any more. No sense dragging insurance companies into this mess. While he was talking to the Prelude guy, Maria and Sheri took Ben and Nicky to the emergency room at Saint Anthony's Hospital. A few stitches and a neck brace for Ben, along with painkillers for both of them. Which couldn't have made the boys happier.

Just before noon the next morning, he returned to the garage with Sheri. They opened the overhead door and examined the Lincoln together. The damage was minimal: a scraped rear bumper, one broken taillight, and a couple of small dents to the bottom of the trunk. But to Alphonse, even the tiniest ding was monumental. After examining the car for a few minutes, Sheri spoke.

"Nicholas and Ben could have been killed, Daddy," she said. "Or you and Mom if you'd driven this to church today."

"The thought crossed my mind," Alphonse responded while still studying the Lincoln.

Sheri seemed about to say something else when she noticed Streeter and an attractive blond woman approaching. Alphonse had called the bounty hunter earlier that morning and asked him to come out to the garage. Told him things had taken another turn toward the serious side the night before: someone bled his brakes and Nicky smashed his car. He sounded like he was about to cry right over the phone, so Streeter said he'd be there by twelve. He said he might be bringing an assistant with him. Watching them walk toward the garage now, Sheri assumed the woman in the tight jeans and navy T-shirt was the assistant her father had mentioned. Figures, she thought. Big, good-looking guy like Streeter would have a plaything like that working for him.

"Look at this, Streeter," the Cheese Man said when they got to him. His voice was as choked and hoarse as that of a chicken with emphysema. "They damn near killed the kid, and my car's half ruined. I got a lot a history with this Lincoln. Lot a history." He looked back at the car and opened his mouth to continue, but instead just shook his head and looked down.

Streeter nodded at Sheri and took a couple of steps into the little garage, which was barely big enough to contain the enormous vehicle, with musty, slightly damp air. Then he turned around and moved back to Alphonse and his daughter in the driveway. For her part, Ronnie just studied the old man and shot an occasional side glance to Sheri.

"That's too bad, Al," Streeter said, "but I think a good repair shop'll be able to get her good as new. I'm more concerned about why it happened." He looked at Ronnie and then at Sheri. "This is my assistant, Ronnie Taggert," he said to Sheri. "She's been giving me a hand, so I thought she should meet you." He looked at Ronnie. "This is Alphonse and Sheri Lucci."

The Cheese Man moved his eyes in her direction but didn't seem really to see her. Sheri just studied her in silence. Ronnie nodded at both of them and smiled.

"How are Nicholas and his friend holding up?" Streeter asked Sheri.

She rolled her eyes. "They were so high that I doubt if they felt a thing when it happened. Ben stayed overnight at the hospital, but that was just for observation. Nicky's pretty stiff in the shoulders today and he has a headache, but he'll live. Maybe this'll get him back into rehab." She paused and looked at the garage again, her shoulders moving up slightly. "But I wouldn't count on it."

"Heck with those two coconuts, Streeter," the old man said suddenly, as if he were just waking up to the whole scene. He turned to the bounty hunter and Ronnie. "If those two kids hadn't come out here last night, it would a been me and Maria in there. Both of us dead, maybe." His head moved from side to side in disbelief. "Maria dead," he concluded weakly.

"Where is she now?" Streeter asked.

"Inside the house packing," Sheri responded. "We're sending her to live with her cousins in Milwaukee until all this is settled. Completely settled."

"That's probably a good idea," Streeter said.

Now Ronnie, looking at Sheri, spoke for the first time.

"Have you and Nicky given any thought to getting away for a while?"

Sheri glanced at her and nodded. "Nicky can't leave the state, so he said he'd go stay with his father up in North-glenn." She rolled her eyes. "The man is useless, but Disanto probably doesn't know about him, and Nicky'll be safe there. I want to tie up a few loose ends and then I'll probably join Mom out in Wisconsin."

"What else can I do?" the Cheese Man asked. "I myself sure ain't running nowhere, but I gotta keep the family safe. Hell, we had the cops out here last night and they talked to all the neighbors. No one saw nothing. Freddy did a real professional job out here. The brake lines were drained and the fluid was taken away. No fluid, no prints, no nothing. One of the cops told me that, an old car like this, I musta forgot to keep the fluid level up. You imagine that? Like I'm senile or something. They did up a traffic-accident report and let it go at that. Plus, the kids were so stoned when the cops got here that that was about all they seemed interested in investigating. Nicholas is lucky they didn't arrest him and his moron buddy." He paused. "The D. didn't leave no trail here."

"Assuming this was Freddy's work," Streeter added.

"Him or Bosco," Alphonse said. "Who else?"

No one spoke for a moment, and then the bounty hunter asked Alphonse, "You given any more thought to selling out to Disanto? It would end all this crap and it might be the smart move."

The Cheese Man shook his head. "I gave it nothing but thought all weekend and I still say no!" His little body shook and his head bobbed in rage. "The day I let that jackass run me outa town is the day I might as well lay down and die."

"Which Freddy might arrange for you," Sheri shot in, obviously mad herself. She turned to Streeter. "We went over it again last night. Over and over. He's not selling and that's that."

Streeter nodded and turned away from them, glancing in the direction of the Lucci house, a few doors to the north. A small white bandage on the back of his head, near the top, covered the glass cut he got Friday morning.

"The hell happened to you?" Alphonse took a step toward him and reached one hand up in the general direction of Streeter's skull.

The bounty hunter turned back and touched the bandage softly. "Someone remodeled my car the other day." He saw the frowns on both Luccis' faces and added, "A couple of my Buick windows got shot out Friday morning. I think it was Mitch Bosco, but I didn't actually see him do it."

"What the hell?" The old man backed away half a step. "Where'd this happen?"

"Out near a junkyard Mitch was visiting." Streeter shifted his weight from his right leg to his left. "I was tailing him like I said I would. Being pretty obvious about it, too. Apparently, he didn't care much for that."

"He tried to kill you?" Sheri stepped forward.

He shrugged. "Probably not. Judging from the sounds of the shots, he was pretty close to my car when he fired. Close enough to hit me if he wanted to. I think this was just his way of trying to scare me off."

"Did it work?" Sheri asked.

"No one scares Tarzan here," Ronnie said. "He didn't even call the police about it. Just took his car in to get the windows replaced and shrugged it off."

"I'll pay for the damage," Alphonse offered. "You followed Bosco, huh?"

Streeter nodded. "Does Ted Kostas mean anything to either of you?"

The old man thought about that for a moment. "I hear the name from time to time. What's he got to do with this?"

"He's the guy who owns the scrap yard Mitch went to. It seems obvious that Kostas knew Mitch took those shots at me." Streeter stared off briefly and then looked back at Al. "First thing tomorrow, I'm going to check out this Mr. Kostas."

"I'll ask around about him this week myself," the old man said. "So what do we do now, Streeter?"

Streeter considered that. "Other than get your family out of the line of fire and check out Kostas, I want to tail Bosco again. I have to get back in the saddle. With someone like Mitch Bosco, you let him think he's won and he has. He and Disanto both have to know I'm hanging in there with you, Al." Streeter nodded and didn't say anything for a moment. "I've got a few other ideas, but I want to discuss them with Frank first."

18

Mitch Bosco sat looking out the eighth-floor sliding glass door of his apartment that Sunday afternoon, studying the Rockies. He had an almost unobstructed view, and it always calmed him to stare at the mountains, some thirty miles away. Earlier he'd gotten a call from a conflicted Freddy Disanto telling him what happened to the Lucci Town Car the night before. Apparently, the D. had gone by Al's place that morning, seen the wrecked Honda, and asked neighbors about it.

"Lucci's idiot grandson tried to take the Lincoln out for a joyride last night and they ended up half totaling another car," Disanto had explained over the phone. "Whoever the hell Ben Champine is, he's got one fucked-up back this morning. And Lucci's grandson, Nicky, ain't feeling just right, either." He paused and Mitch could hear him wheezing slightly into the receiver. "I swear, that old Cheese

Man's made outa Teflon. Nothing ever sticks to him. This is like West Vail all over again."

"Now, wait a minute," Mitch had come back. "I did what you said, where you said, and exactly when you said to do it. This was no mistake by me." No sir, he thought. Freddy Disanto set up this boner by himself. Serves the big jerk right. Drives me over to the garage on Friday night like I'm a damned ten-year-old.

"Am I blaming you?" Freddy said loudly. "Did you hear me blame you? Hell, getting the kid is almost as good as if the old man was in the car. Lucci got the message. Especially after I called him a while ago to say I heard about the accident and that I couldn't be more sorry. I even hinted that we should get together and talk about his selling price on the pizza joint, strongly suggesting that he had enough on his mind without worrying about his various family members and their general health and safety. He knew it was me that set it up after I got that one in." The D. paused. "It's just that the old man keeps dodging the bullets. That's all."

"Okay, then." Bosco eased off some. "How did the old guy react to your mentioning the restaurant business?"

"First he sounded like he just found a dead rat in his minestrone." Freddy was smiling now. "Then he said he'd get back to me on it. I tell you what, Mitchie. Something like this, it first looks like a screwup and then turns out it might be the best thing that could have happened."

Mitch considered that for a moment. "It's like Anthony Robbins teaches: Treat every failure as a learning opportunity. Remember, the people with the most success are usually the ones who failed the most."

Freddy frowned into the phone. "Yeah, it's just like that. I'll talk to you later this week." With that he hung up.

Now, still staring at the Rockies, Mitch contemplated the second call he'd received that afternoon. It was from one of the Arizona financial backers. The guy—he would only give his name as Niles—had called Mitch twice in the past week. Evidently, Freddy the D. had told him he was working with Bosco "on our Lucci difficulties" and Niles called to get a progress update.

"Our faith in Mr. Disanto has been shaken," Niles had told him in their first conversation. "You can understand that, given how long it's taking Mr. Disanto and still he hasn't come to terms with Mr. Lucci."

Mitch played along, especially after Niles mentioned that if he could speed things up the Arizona associates might be inclined to reward him with a piece of the action once the development was finished. He, Mitch, could manage the project rather than Freddy Disanto, as was originally planned. So today Mitch told him that they were sensing some flexibility in Alphonse's position, now that his family was drawn deeply into the negotiating process.

This pleased Niles no end, since Freddy had told him months ago that Lucci's daughter favored the deal all along. Niles then concluded by saying that, if something fatal were to happen to the elder Lucci and Sheri were to take control of his properties, well, sir, they'd probably get their deal on the spot. The notion of a dead Al Lucci wasn't wasted on Mitch for a second. But he asked why Niles and his friends didn't just pass that idea directly on to Disanto. He was reminded, "We simply have lost faith in Mr. Disanto's ability to get the job done. Besides, it sounds as though you would be the man to do the actual work. No point getting too many people involved in a project like that."

Hot damn. Squeeze the D. right on out of the picture. Mitch was all for that. No more being called Mitchie. No more looking at that ugly ape and hearing his guttural orders. Mitch would be the man in Denver. Now, that would be a long entry for his "Prosperity Journal." And killing old man Lucci would be easy enough to arrange, Mitch realized as he walked to the kitchen for a hit of ginger schnapps. The hard part would be dealing with Freddy the D. if Mitch were to take over his spot with the Arizona financial backers. That would require some serious thought.

19

Mitch thought he was seeing a ghost that Monday morning. Crazy bounty hunter had his piece-of-junk Buick all fixed up good as new and was back on Mitch's butt by about nine. Everywhere he went for over three hours: the bank, the supermarket, the downtown library, to T.K. Scrap for a quick stop. All the way to his coffee meeting just after lunchtime. He didn't think Streeter had followed him into the restaurant itself, and he wasn't waiting outside afterward. Which was fine with Mitch. Maybe the big man was finally taking a break.

"How's your newest bestest buddy?" Ronnie asked Streeter when they settled into Frank's office shortly before two o'clock that day. "You're not going to be needing any new windows on that classic vehicle of yours, are you?"

"Not today," he answered. "But I think Mitch is starting

to warm up to me. At least he didn't throw any shots at me this morning."

"Let's get down to business, Miss Ronnie," Frank said softly as he rocked behind his desk. "Did you find out anything interesting when you checked on Kostas over at Denver court this morning?"

"He's another winner, only more so," she answered. "Ted Kostas is every bit as hopeless as the rest of the bunch. Nine arrests. Basically for the same nickel-and-dime stuff that Bosco gets involved in. Apparently Ted is a fence for stolen goods, and he's proficient if not all that successful." She nodded to a stack of papers on Frank's desk. "You can read all about it in there. Only four convictions, so he must have a decent lawyer. But the guy is a twenty-four-karat loser. His most recent bust was a few months ago, when he tried to solicit an undercover policewoman for sex at Big Danny's on South Federal. He must like strip clubs."

Streeter glanced at Frank. "You know Danny Fisk, don't you?"

The bondsman nodded. "I've written up a few of his bouncers when they got carried away doing their jobs. They get the occasional assault charge. Danny's an all-right guy."

"Anyhow," Ronnie continued, "Kostas seems to work alone, and he's run that junkyard or whatever it is for years. Apparently he does a lot of his fencing out of there. Never been married, at least never divorced, and he's had two DUIs over the past fifteen years. A lot of assorted other traffic violations, and he's been sued several times for late payments to different people."

"I'm meeting up with Al for dinner at his house, and maybe he'll have more on Kostas then," Streeter interjected.

"So the question to us is, what business does Mitch Bosco have with Mr. Kostas?" Frank asked. He stopped rocking and looked at the two people across from him. "Any ideas?"

"It might be that Kostas has something to do with Mitch and the cops," Streeter responded. "Carey said he's helping the police, and when I followed him to the Rocky Mountain Diner a little while ago, Bosco sat down with a young couple at a booth by the window. I don't think anyone saw me standing outside of the place, but the woman looked familiar. I've seen here in court, at a couple of bond hearings, and if memory serves me, I think she's a deputy DA. I don't know her name, but she's definitely with the DA's office. It's interesting that Mitch went to meet her right after he made a short stop at Kostas's place."

"Could be Teddy's involved with whatever Mitch and the cops are doing, all right," Frank said, leaning forward.

Streeter nodded. "I'd sure like to find out." He thought for a moment. "Could you give Danny Fisk a call today and see if he knows much about Kostas?"

"Sure," his partner said.

"Why?" Ronnie asked.

"Maybe no good reason," Streeter said. "Let's wait and see what Danny says. I might have an idea as to how to get inside Kostas's head."

"That sounds like a lonely place to be," Ronnie shot back.

"Probably, but I'd still like to know how he fits in with Bosco," Streeter said. "If Kostas is a regular at Danny's, then I think I have a way we can get to him."

"How's that?" Frank asked.

"Let's just wait until you talk to Danny." He turned to Ronnie. "Are you busy this afternoon?"

She looked to Frank, who shook his head. "I guess not. Why?"

"Go over to the secretary of state's office and look up the filings on Disanto & Associates, Inc. Al told me the other day that that's what Freddy said his company is named. He mentioned it way back when he first started asking about buying up the pizza joint. I'd like to know who's in bed with Freddy on this project. Get copies of all the paperwork. Maybe we can approach his partners."

"And do what?" Frank asked.

"How the heck do I know?" The bounty hunter sounded a little irritated. "I just want to find out who we're dealing with here. It seems like a lead-pipe cinch that there has to be some brains behind Disanto and Bosco."

"You going to go lean on them and get all heavy, like you did with Disanto last week?" Frank frowned. "Hassling a stone-cold killer like that. Not a terrifically intelligent move there, Street."

"Enough about that, okay? I may have done some good with the guy, and if we can get more names, maybe we can get to those people, too. Let his partners know that we know who they are. It could cause problems for Disanto and Bosco, and that's about the best strategy I can come up with for right now." Streeter paused. "There's so much about this situation that doesn't make any sense. Like who set up that robbery at Al's card game last week?"

"That would be a sixty-four-thousand-dollar question," Frank agreed.

"It sure is, along with finding out what Mitch Bosco has going with the police," Streeter said.

Ronnie stood up. "Do you get this involved in all of your cases?"

He frowned. "What do you mean?"

"Oh, let's see. Working seven days a week on a case. Getting shot at. Talking about it until all hours."

He shrugged and looked up at her. "Doesn't everyone work like this?"

"No. But that's okay. I didn't mean it as a criticism." Ronnie picked up a legal pad from the desk. "It means you care. I just wonder why you care so much about the Luccis. They're not what you'd call pillars of the community."

He shrugged. "Maybe I do have an emotional attachment to the case. There's something about old Al. He's sort of pathetic, but in a charming way. All of his posturing at first, and yet he's about as hard as sponge cake. I know he's not always aboveboard, but he's really not a bad man. I get the same vibe from him as I did from my father. You know, the tough-guy front with nothing like that on the inside. I was too young to do my father any good. He died when I was a teenager, so I never knew him as an adult. Helping little Al makes me feel like I'm doing something I'd like to have done for my old man."

"How'd he die?" Ronnie's voice softened.

"He drank a lot. Smoked about a carton of cigarettes every day, and he never cared much about eating. He died of old age and he was only in his mid-fifties. His body just gave out." Now he stood up. "Plus, there's another very concrete reason I'm working this case so hard. Money. Al gave me another five grand yesterday. Let's go earn it, Ronnie."

20

The minute Mitch walked into the restaurant, Karen Maples could see that he was jumpy. Not a lot, but the guy was definitely rattled. The fringe of long hair around his bare white scalp looked rumpled, like he'd been running his hands through it. His eyes were a smudged red and they were hopping around the room, trying to take in too much. He worked his mouth silently, as if his teeth itched. Just great, she thought. Less than a week to go and this boob's getting unhinged on me.

"Over here, cowboy." She said it just a tad above her normal voice, but there was enough spine in it to grab his attention.

Bosco frowned in confusion. When he recognized the lawyer and her assistant—Todd something-or-other—he straightened his shoulders and moved toward them. They were sitting in a north, window-wall booth at the Rocky Mountain Diner, an upscale place near the federal courthouse downtown. Mitch had eaten there a couple of times and he loved the buffalo meatloaf. But food was not much on his mind this particular afternoon.

"Hey, Miss Maples," he said when he got to the booth. His eyes were fixed on Karen's, ignoring Todd. He winked at her awkwardly and held out his hand to be shaken. He'd read a hundred times about the importance of maintaining eye contact and sounding sincere. The presentation of confidence is everything.

"You can skip what I assume you're trying to pass off as charm and just sit down." Karen nodded to the seat across from her and Todd without shaking Mitch's hand.

Bosco could see there was little point in trying to win her over, but he didn't feel inclined to give in to her, either. "How are you today?"

"Outstanding. Okay, Mitch?" Karen stared hard at him as he eased into the booth. "I need to get a few things straight with you. Just do me a favor and don't act like we're old friends. After this weekend, we're probably not ever going to talk to each other again. At least not outside of your plea and sentencing, and that's strictly business."

"This weekend?" Mitch asked as casually as he could. That was fine with him—never talking to this one again. Look at her over there, he thought. Chubby little dictator. Fairly plain face with too much makeup and wearing those expensive girl-suits with the padded shoulders.

Karen nodded. "Right. Things are in place for the Kostas sting and there's no point in waiting."

Just then the waitress appeared with a menu and ice water for Mitch. He waved away the menu. "Don't need that," he said. "Coffee and cream'll do it."

The waitress glanced at Todd and Karen. "More for you, too?"

Karen shook her head. "We'll be leaving soon."

Mitch leaned forward, putting his elbows on the table and resting his chin in his folded hands. "You sound a little rushed."

She ignored the comment. "Listen to me, Mitch. Listen good. Todd here has the Jaguars lined up. Or, rather, he will by Friday. Both of them. You hook him up with Teddy Kostas before then. Todd will set up the sale for the next night. Saturday." She paused. "Teddy's still hot for this thing, isn't he?"

Mitch nodded.

"Good. And he's got his cash ready?"

"So he says. I told him we'd be asking fifteen apiece for them. That number's big enough that it makes sense, but small enough that he can get the cash and turn the cars over for a good profit. I think he has them sold for about thirty-five thousand each. And he told me just now that he's got the buyers ready anytime he gets the Jags. He's creaming in his pants for the deal." Mitch paused. "If you'll pardon my language."

"Outstanding, Mitch." Karen ignored his last comment and took a sip from her coffee, keeping the cup up near face level after she finished. "We're going to work fast and hard. You don't have to know the details, but Todd's going to try and snare the buyers while he's at it."

"Whatever works." Mitch glanced at Todd. "When you want to meet him?"

Todd shifted in his seat and cleared his throat. "Thursday."

Mitch studied the investigator for a moment. Then he returned his attention to the prosecutor. "And my deal is all wired for court on Monday? You're going to recommend probation, right?"

"I want to talk to you about that."

Mitch frowned deeply but said nothing.

"Here's the thing, Bosco. I've put enough work into Kostas and we're too close for me to let some idiot screw it up now." She paused and sat back a bit. "I've been getting all sorts of shit from the guys in Narcotics lately. They say you're doing a bit of business in the area of drugs and they don't understand why they can't pop you. Now, I've held them off so far, but I'm tired of it." She took a deep breath and let that sink in.

"Tired enough that I'm getting the word to Narcotics this afternoon that it's a green light to nail you if they get a chance. Starting now. Our deal with you is for the arrest on the gun-running charge. If you get popped for drugs this week, believe me, Bosco, I'll personally prosecute you. And I guarantee you that I'll get a conviction and I'll ask for the max. You combine that with me asking the max on the gun charges if you foul up this sting by getting arrested and, well, hell, cowboy, you'll die in prison. Seeing to it that that happens will be my personal mission in life. I want Ted Kostas. I want him badly. But if you do anything to jeopardize that sting, I'll forget all about him and go after you like I've never gone after anyone." She shot her eyebrows up. "Are you getting all this?"

Mitch had leaned back a tad himself as she spoke, unconsciously wiping his open right hand down the front of his T-shirt. Finally, he spoke. "I hear you."

Karen shook her head slowly a couple of times and then nodded. "Just so we understand each other. Actually, I don't understand you at all, but that's not important. Just so long as you know where I'm coming from." She leaned in and lowered her voice. "Straight from hell, as far as you're concerned. I mean it, Bosco. I'm done covering for you with Narcotics."

By now Mitch was really depressed: Streeter following him all over the place and Maples threatening him like he was a schoolboy. Still, he managed a thin smile. "The wisdom to create a plan and keep to it is the key to any business success."

"Put a lid on that kind of thing," Karen said, shaking her head. "Just keep your nose clean. At least until Kostas is taken down. After you get Todd in place, your business is no longer my business."

"I'm not sure what those Narcotics guys are feeding you, but you won't have to worry about me moving anything ever again." Mitch knew that was true. If he could get solid with Niles and the people in Arizona, he'd never go near a coke deal for the rest of his life.

"Whatever," Karen said with little enthusiasm. Then she glanced at Todd and nodded.

"I'll call you sometime Thursday, so stick around the phone until you hear from me," Todd told Mitch evenly. There was no emotion in his voice; he seldom paid attention to Mitch. "In the meantime, let Kostas know you and me'll be coming over to see him with one of the cars on Friday. I want him to view the merchandise and know who he'll be dealing with. I have to have his trust."

"I can do that," Mitch said. "I let him know this morning that he'd be seeing one of the cars real soon."

"Outstanding, Mitch," Karen interjected. "But try and get some sleep before Friday, okay? You look like hell."

21

It was a toss-up as to which tore Alphonse Lucci apart more: calling off his weekly poker game that night or taking Maria to the airport late that afternoon. Both had been such a big part of his life for so long. Still, he struggled to put on a brave front as he showed Streeter into the kitchen of his home shortly before six o'clock for a lasagna dinner and Chianti.

"Nothing like the old bachelor life, huh, Streeter?" He plastered on an open-mouthed grin, but the rest of his face didn't go along with it. Alphonse hadn't spent more than a week, total, away from Maria in the entire forty-seven years they'd been married, and he had no idea how'd he make it through the night without her around. Sure, they slept in separate rooms, but at least he knew she was there for him. Knew she was safe, too. In his green-and-yellow plaid shirt and brown corduroy pants, all about two sizes too large, he looked very alone and vulnerable.

"I should a thought a this years ago," he said as he bent

over the oven to check the lasagna. Then he straightened up and looked at his guest, the smile still in place. His head bobbed slightly as he spoke. "You care for a little *vino?*"

Streeter glanced at the large bottle of Chianti on the sink. The room had the subdued professional-garlic odor of a fine restaurant, and he knew this would be one killer of a meal.

"Sure, Al." Streeter paused. "What time was Maria's flight?"

The smile dropped from Alphonse's face and his head lowered. "I don't know. Three-something. Damned drive out to DIA takes forever." His head moved down farther. "Seemed like the drive coming home takes about twice that."

"She'll be back in no time, Al," Streeter said as he walked to the sink and picked up the wine bottle. "This thing can't go on forever. Where do you keep the glasses?"

The old man nodded toward the shelves to the right of the sink, but he was obviously lost in thought. Streeter grabbed two juice glasses and set them next to the Chianti. "And the opener?"

Al didn't seem to hear him at first but after a moment he responded. "It's already been opened. Just pull the cork out." He studied Streeter and then added, "How we doing with this Disanto thing, Streeter? You come up with anything new?"

The bounty hunter nodded. "Maybe. I've got to figure out a few details, but I'm working on a way that'll hopefully get us to Ted Kostas." He picked up the Chianti and the glasses. "Bosco went over to see him this morning and from there he went on to meet with a deputy DA for lunch. I don't know what they talked about, but my hunch is Kostas figures in with whatever Mitch is doing with the cops."

The old man considered that for a moment and then nodded to the wine in Streeter's hand. "You gonna pour us a little, or you just want to stand there holding that thing all night?"

Streeter glanced at the bottle and then at the two glasses in his other hand. He shrugged and set the glasses on the counter, filled them with the Chianti, and handed one to Alphonse.

"Thanks, Streeter," the Cheese Man said as he took his glass. "I made a few calls on the Greek today. Kostas. He's an old ham-and-egger from way back. Mostly he fences stolen property, but he'll dabble in darn near anything to turn a buck. Other than that, I can't tell you much. Fairly harmless in the sense of hurting people, and no brains to speak of. That's the word I got." He studied his guest. "You say you don't know his connection to Mitch? That might be nice to find out."

"You got that right." He held up his glass in a quick salute and then took a sip. "Like I said, I'm working on a way to do it. It'll happen in the next day or so. I'm also going to be doing some digging into the people Disanto is working with on that West Side block development. The one with your pizza restaurant. I don't know what we'll find, but I want to put the pressure on anyone near Disanto."

"Makes sense." Alphonse paused. "It would also be nice to find out who set up that thing with the Ramirez Boys last week. I can't believe it was Disanto. Him getting bopped on the head and robbed like that, and then going after one of them."

"I figure, if we can get to everyone, sooner or later we'll nail that one down, too." Streeter glanced at the oven. "That smells great, Al."

"What do you expect from this kitchen?" The old man opened the oven door and studied the pan of lasagna inside. Without a word, he grabbed two large pot holders from the counter and pulled the pan out. "We'll let it cool down some and then it's time to eat," he told the bounty hunter. His voice seemed sad again, as it had when he'd talked about Maria.

"You okay, Al?" Streeter asked.

The Cheese Man's head bobbed as he picked up his glass of wine. "I guess so." Then he took a step toward his guest and looked long and hard into his eyes. "I gotta ask you, Streeter. You think I'm full a shit not selling to Disanto? I mean, that restaurant has a lot of sentimental value and all that, but is it worth people getting killed over? That guy in Wyoming. Maybe Nicky and his idiot friend the other night. Tell me the truth. Am I just being a stubborn old fart here or what?"

"You are being that," Streeter said with a hint of a smile. "No doubt about it. And I'd sell if I was you. You'd still have the catering business here and in Vail and your other pizza joint. Not to mention the money from Freddy." He paused and put a hand on Alphonse's shoulder. "But it's your restaurant and you shouldn't have to sell if you don't want to. Plus, Disanto's got his personal reasons to make life bad for you. This isn't all about business."

"You might be right there." Al nodded slowly. "Just so I can keep the family safe." He looked back up at Streeter. "I don't care for myself so much. It's Maria and the rest a them." Alphonse glanced back at the lasagna. "Let's eat."

They were about halfway through dinner when the phone rang. At first, Alphonse just looked at it, on the wall over next to the refrigerator. Finally, he got up and answered it.

"Yeah?" he greeted the caller. "Sheri. Where are you?" He listened for a while, frowning at what was being said. Then: "I'll be right over. Yeah, right now." With that, he hung up and turned back to the table. He looked like he was about to cry.

"What's wrong, Al?" Streeter stood up.

The little man looked over at him and his mouth opened but nothing came out. Then he tried again. "It's Nicky. He's in the hospital. Sounds like he's dying. Can you do me a favor? Get me to Saint Anthony's right now, okay?"

22

Actually, Nicholas Lucci was nowhere near dead by the time Alphonse and Streeter got to Saint Anthony's. In fact, he'd been moved from Intensive Care and upgraded to serious but stable. Around four that afternoon, Nicholas had become conscious briefly and had been slipping in and out of it for the past few hours. It turned out that he'd been partying with a girl he knew, and they had both overdosed on all the fun. Jack Daniel's and Demerol. Shortly before noon, Nicky and his friend were rushed to the hospital. Both had their stomachs pumped and both would pull through. Sheri had waited on calling Alphonse at least until the boy was out of trouble, but she'd still sounded extremely upset.

Of course, Alphonse didn't know Nicholas was okay as they drove to the hospital. By the time they pulled up to the emergency-room entrance, the old man could barely breathe. He did his own feeble version of jumping out of the car, which almost cost him a broken ankle as he caught his foot on the door on the way out. Stumbling forward, arms flailing, he took all the way to the front door to steady himself. Then he ran inside, grabbed the first nurse he could find, and demanded to know where his grandson was. The two of them along with a clerk in admittance needed twenty minutes to figure out what happened. When he realized that Nicholas was all right, the old man didn't know if he was more relieved or mad at his daughter and her son for throwing such a big scare into him.

By this time, Streeter had parked the car and made it to the front lobby, where Alphonse sat panting on one of the huge overstuffed couches. "Is the boy okay?" Streeter asked.

The Cheese Man just nodded a couple of times and waved broadly with his left hand, apparently indicating that he needed breathing room.

Streeter studied the old man. "I think you should get examined by one of the doctors yourself. You're not looking very good, Al."

Alphonse gulped air and glanced up at him. "Give me a break, okay? I come running down here thinking the kid's all but dead and then I find out he's upstairs eating Jell-O and playing Nintendo or whatever. A regular roller-coaster is what I been on here. You can see that." He paused and sucked in some more air. "I tell you one thing, that daughter a mine shows her face down here, she'll be the one needs an ER."

"Is that right, Daddy?" Sheri's voice came from behind Streeter. Both Alphonse and he spun around in her direction. "Here I think I did you a favor by waiting to call and this is the thanks I get?"

The old man's head continued to move back and forth as he breathed loudly through his mouth and stared at her. Streeter's face said nothing and he stepped off to the side to let her approach her father.

"You want thanks?" Alphonse asked in a deep wheeze.

"Scare the living crap out a me and you want thanks?" He glanced off in confusion. Suddenly, he looked back up at her and asked sharply, "Was this Bosco and the D. again?"

Sheri studied him for a long moment and finally shook her head. "Nicky said he was drinking Jack Daniel's with this little girl he's been running around with. She broke out the Demerol and they went for some downer cocktails. They were at the girl's apartment, and the only thing that saved them was that her roommate came home for lunch and found them. Everyone's okay, but they're both sicker than all hell."

The Cheese Man nodded slowly. "It's like he's trying to kill himself." He leaned forward as if he was going to stand up. "Is all this drug garbage supposed to be fun? Nearly kill yourself for kicks. What's he thinking about anyhow?"

"Why don't you go ask him?" Sheri nodded her head to the side, toward the elevators. "He's conscious and he's been asking for you."

Alphonse stood up.

"One good thing might have come out of all this," Sheri said before he moved any farther. "Nicky told me he'll go to Hazelden. Right away, before his next trial. The court should let him do that. He wants the whole sixty-day inpatient treatment. That's the first time he ever said that he'd go to rehab. He's leaving right away, tomorrow morning."

The old man considered that and then broke into a weak smile. He and Sheri had investigated the drug-and-alcohol rehabilitation center in Minnesota, but every time they mentioned it to Nicholas, he would either yell at them or withdraw. "Then this wasn't so bad, after all," he told Sheri. With that he headed for the elevators.

Sheri and Streeter watched him get into one and then just stood there silently in the large lobby. After a while, she turned and faced Streeter, who was standing about four feet away, looking calm, his hands in his back pockets.

"How'd you get dragged into this?" she asked him.

"I was having dinner with Al when you called." He took his hands out of his pockets and stepped up to her. Sheri wasn't wearing much makeup, and she looked more tired and older than he'd ever seen her. "So you don't think Nicholas was trying to kill himself."

"No more than usual. Do you want to get a cup of coffee? There's a cafeteria just over there a ways."

"I'm pretty coffeed up right now, but I'll sit with you for a bit."

They headed down a wide hall. Sheri was wearing tight jeans and a white T-shirt. Tired or not, she had the figure of a woman a solid ten years younger. One who worked out, at that. Her hair was longer and darker than Streeter recalled, and she smelled faintly like body lotion. When they arrived, he got a table in the corner and she went for coffee. The room tried to disguise itself with subdued lighting and art prints, but it still felt like a hospital. Faintly antiseptic, full of hushed conversations.

"This *is* a blessing in disguise," Sheri said when she sat down across from him. She stirred her coffee and looked up at him. "Nicky going for inpatient rehab. I guess having your stomach pumped can change your outlook. Between that and the car business Saturday, Nicky's getting the message that he can't dodge the bullet forever."

Her eyes looked sad and she didn't have any edge in her voice.

Streeter began, "Why do you think he's so . . ."

"Fucked up?" she interrupted. "I don't mean to sound vulgar, but let's not beat around the bush." She paused. "I might not be mother of the year, but I tried to do the best I could for him. And Lord knows his grandmother gave him enough love. But when he was little, his useless father and I were pretty caught up in the whole drug thing ourselves.

Pot, pills, and partying. Nicky got used to being ignored, and when his father left, well, it tore him up. Nicky worshiped the man. I think he's trying to get back at me for driving him off." She took a long drink from her coffee. "That's the best I can come up with, anyhow. Do you have any kids, Streeter?"

"No."

"Never been married, huh?"

He broke into a grin. "I've just never been married long enough to start a family."

"That's a shame." Sheri waved one hand casually around the room. "See what you're missing?" Her eyes bored in on his. "Do you have a girlfriend?"

The bounty hunter leaned back in his chair and frowned. "Not at the moment."

"How long has 'the moment' been?"

"Why?"

"Just curious." Sheri smiled. "You're very appealing and I assume you're straight, so I was just wondering why you're not attached."

"Well, the moment's been a few months, but let's change the subject."

Sheri nodded, leaned into the table, and yawned. "I'll be leaving with Nicky in the morning, too. I'll get him settled in at Hazelden, and then I'm driving over to stay with Mom in Milwaukee. It's about a six-hour drive, so I can go visit Nicky from time to time."

"That's probably a good idea." Streeter shifted his weight in his seat. "I just hope it doesn't take us sixty days to get Disanto and Bosco in line. I don't think your father could stand that much pressure and suspense. Not to mention being away from your mother for that long."

"Then hurry up and take care of Freddy. Okay, Streeter?" There was no humor in her voice.

23

"So, Danny says he'll play ball with us?" Streeter asked Frank. He'd just finished telling him and Ronnie about his night at the hospital. He was sitting casually on the bondsman's credenza that Tuesday morning, his legs dangling in front of him. Frank relaxed, swiveling in his huge chair; Ronnie sat upright in one of the visitors' chairs across the desk, staring at both of them.

"Turns out he'd be happy to give us a hand with this bozo," Frank finally responded. "He tells me that old Ted Kostas is a royal pain in the neck. Comes in practically every night drunk, nurses a cheap beer for hours, never tips Danny's girls, and generally makes a pest of himself. Half the time the bouncers end up telling him to leave. Danny says the only reason he doesn't bar the guy for life is because he sometimes brings in friends and he never gets violent. Danny'll help us, for sure."

"Good." Streeter got off the credenza and stood up.

"We've got to get something out of Ted, and I figure the best way to do that is through his weakness for women of the strip-club variety. If Danny'll let us put a woman on the inside, maybe we can get Kostas to open up a little."

Frank leaned forward in his chair and put his elbows on his knees. "That could work, Street. But we'll have to use a lady with a lot of sizzle. One who's hot and still can keep her wits about her. She'll have to have raw nerve, too. Danny's place is pretty down and dirty. I've been there a few times and it's definitely not for the fainthearted. Not to mention that this is pretty much of a long shot, even if we had someone like that available."

Streeter nodded. "That it is. If you've got a better plan, I'd love to let hear it." He walked around the desk toward Ronnie. "But I already know the woman for the job."

Ronnie turned herself in her chair to watch him. "I'll just bet you do, Streeter."

"We're back to 'Streeter' again." His eyes got all wide and innocent. "Anyhow, you're perfect for this, Ronnie. All that training in Chicago at getting lonely men to open up. This is the role you were born to play."

She looked at Frank and shook her head, although she didn't appear to be mad. "Whores for hire, that's me. The more down and dirty, the better."

The bondsman sat up and looked at both of them. "You're thinking Miss Ronnie here, huh? This is pretty far beyond the call of duty and you know it."

"Not that far," Streeter said softly, moving between Ronnie and the desk, and then staring down straight into her eyes. "If this was Disanto or maybe even Bosco, I'd say it was too risky. But Kostas is fairly harmless." He paused. "Anyhow, if you don't want to do it, Ronnie, I'll understand. But we'll keep an eye on you the whole time. Just pretend Kostas is a wayward husband and you're nailing down the goods. You were the one who wanted to get into the PI business. Sometimes we have to do pretense work like this."

"That's a nice way to put it." Ronnie stood up and nodded. She was wearing a loose black sweatshirt over tight washed-out jeans. "You know there's no way I'd turn you down, don't you?"

"That was my assumption. Plus, Danny's isn't all that seedy."

"I can just imagine," she said. "It's probably fun for the whole family—right, Street?"

He shot her a wink. "I'm glad we're back to 'Street' again."

"How we going to wire it?" Frank asked.

Streeter turned to his partner. "You call Danny Fisk and tell him he's got a new waitress for tonight. Or tomorrow night, or whenever he thinks Bosco's likely to come into his place next. Tell him that she's experienced and she'll work cheap. Free, in fact. Think he'll go for that?"

Frank nodded. "Probably. He owes me a favor or two, and when I tell him about Miss Ronnie here"—he nodded at her—"Big Danny'll jump at the offer."

Streeter then turned back to Ronnie. "Dress up in your best stray-husband clothes and plan on spending some time working the tables. Frank will have Danny point out Kostas to you, and then you go wait on him. Get him interested in you, which shouldn't be all that difficult. I want you to get him to ask you to sit down for a drink. Better still, if he comes on to you, tell him you get off soon and you'll meet him somewhere else. Somewhere quiet for a drink. Make it a public place, like an appropriate bar where you can have a little privacy and still be seen at all times. Charlie Brown's in Capitol Hill could work. It's never too crowded and it should suit Bosco." He turned to Frank again. "Maybe

Danny can use you as a bartender at his place, too, so you can keep an eye on them while they're inside." Then, back to Ronnie: "I'll be out in the car and I'll follow you to Charlie Brown's. He knows what I look like, so I can't be in the room with you two. But I can wait outside in the car to make sure you're not getting in over your head."

"What if he wants to go somewhere real quiet?" Ronnie asked. "Like, say, his apartment."

"You can't let that happen." Streeter studied her. "Insist on meeting him at a public bar and I'm sure he'll be so thrilled at the offer that he won't complain. Take your own car to Charlie Brown's and tell him you'll follow him there. If he gets weird about it, the whole thing's off. No way I'm putting you in that kind of a spot. You don't go to his place alone with him under any circumstances."

Ronnie looked at Streeter like she had another question. Then she nodded. "I hear you, boss. If I didn't know better I'd say you were getting jealous on me."

Streeter frowned. "Yeah, right. I've seen this guy, and if he's your type, I won't stand in the way of your happiness."

"How you going to handle him?" Frank asked her.

"The same way I'd handle any other guy, only more so." Ronnie sat back down in the chair and ran a hand through her hair. "Smile, show him some cleavage, and act like what he says is important. Butter up his ego. I'll just play it out for all it's worth. I know what we're looking for and I can be very subtle *and* persistent at the same time."

"Sounds good," Streeter said. "We'll go over the details more if and when we set this up." Then he turned to Frank. "You better get on the horn to Danny as soon as possible. Let him know we won't cause him any problems and he'll get free help for part of the night."

The bondsman nodded. "He'll go along with us."

"Good." Streeter moved away from the desk. "Ronnie, how'd you make out at the secretary of state's office yesterday on Disanto & Associates?"

She picked up her notebook from the desk and studied it. "I don't know if I did you much good. For the corporate officers, the articles of incorporation listed just Disanto and a woman's name, Angie Disanto, who I assume is his wife or daughter. They both have the same address. The registered agent is an attorney down on 17th, but he probably doesn't know anything about Freddy's activities.

"There's also a Niles Macmillan listed on the papers as a corporate officer. Vice-president, no less. His address is a P.O. box in Scottsdale." She looked up at Streeter. "No phone number or anything else for Niles, so I went to the library and got a Phoenix phone book. They don't have a listing for his residence. I also called Directory Assistance for Macmillan's home phone, but it's unlisted. But there was a Macmillan Development Company in the directory." She pointed to the notebook. "The number's written out there."

"Good work."

"Very thorough, Miss Ronnie," Frank put in. "Lots of initiative there."

"She'll need it when she works Kostas," Streeter said, moving toward the door. "Look, I've got some errands to run downtown this morning. Get a hold of Danny as soon as you can. Okay, Frank?"

Frank nodded.

"You seem to be more hurried than usual about this thing," Ronnie said.

"I keep thinking of old Al last night." Streeter's voice was softer now. "He's not going to hold up all that much longer with Disanto on his tail and Maria out of town. And his family's on me to take care of this mess. I want us to get to Kostas and get to him fast. Then I want to call Niles what's-his-name in Arizona and see if he knows what the D. is doing up here with Alphonse."

"And what if he does?" Ronnie asked.

"Then I'll give him the same line I gave Disanto about going to the cops with it. Someone, somewhere along the line, has to break down and call off Freddy and Mitch."

24

Ronnie Taggert was dressed so hot that Wednesday night that in less than two hours of waiting tables she made over a hundred fifty dollars in tips. In the first hour, a few of the regular waitresses were getting jealous, and by nine-thirty, almost all of them were visibly upset with her. She was even getting more attention than most of the dancers. Big Danny Fisk offered her a full-time job on the spot. Frank, seeing that she was just playing a role and enjoying it, beamed at her from behind the bar. And Streeter, well, he flat-out had no idea what to make of her. When she pulled up to the church in her Celica to follow him to the strip club on South Federal Boulevard, he only saw her head, face, and upper body. That was provocative enough. Her hair teased up, heavy makeup, and a red Danskin top tight enough to threaten suffocation.

But it was when she parked behind the club and got out of her car that Streeter really had to stop and think. Black skirt high and snug. At first, he thought it was her belt. Fishnet stockings with heels so tall and skinny she seemed to be teetering on swizzle sticks. And the look on her face really shook him: her eyes moody and her mouth pouting. Plus, her head seemed to sway ever so slightly, as if she was enjoying a private fantasy with whomever she was looking at.

Ted Kostas didn't have a chance. He arrived at Big Danny's shortly after ten—slightly plastered and frisky, as Danny had described. When Ronnie dipped at his table to serve him his beer, she threw him a come-on grin that almost melted his metal Zippo lighter. He nodded, came back with his own version of a smile, and then threw an extra seventy-five cents on her tray. A real stretch for the fat man.

"You new here, honey?" Ted asked her before she left his table. He was wearing a soiled tan-and-gray flannel shirt that sagged over his belt with the weight of his thick and lumpy stomach. Old blue jeans and work boots completed his ensemble, and even from a few feet away, he smelled like a used ashtray. "I never seen you around before." He batted his bloodshot gray eyes which seemed to drift around with a mind of their own.

Ronnie's eyes widened for a second as she put the change in her tip tray. Then she winked. "I'm new, but this isn't my first night. Thanks, Big Time." With that, she turned away.

"Hold on there, honey," Ted said, reaching up and grabbing her by the elbow. He gave it a quick but firm tug and held it. "No need to be in such a big hurry to rush off like that. I'm what you might call a preferred customer around here."

She raised an eyebrow. "And why is that?"

"Because . . ." His voice trailed off for a few seconds. Then he recovered. "Because I'm here more than anyone else."

When he got that out, a lame smile crossed his face, causing his beard to lift and his eyes to crinkle as though he were in pain. "And I know how to treat a broad." He concluded with a deep cough. And then another.

Ronnie glanced him. "Aren't you ever the hopeless romantic?"

He nodded and looked around the room. The sound system was blaring generic hard rock. Plenty of thump and bite. In fact, Danny's was pretty much generic blue-collar throughout. Three stages, each with shiny dancing poles and background mirror. Two long bars to make sure no one had to wait, with the rest of the place kept dark enough to give the constant feeling that it was past midnight all over the world. The woman on the stage closest to them was doing her rendition of the splits, although when she bottomed out she struggled not to tip over. Ted looked back at Ronnie.

"I try to be, but if I can't be that, at least I can be exciting." He let out a wheezy grunt, half a laugh and half a cough.

She leaned in toward him slightly. "I'll bet."

Her voice was husky enough that Ted had to swallow hard. "What's your name?"

"You can call me Lesley. And you?"

"You can call me Uncle Ted." With that, he slipped into an awkward silence, clearly uncomfortable having an actual conversation with one of the waitresses.

Ronnie shifted her weight from one leg to the other and waited. When it became apparent that the guy had no more rap, she spoke. "Well, Uncle Ted, I'm off in about twenty minutes."

Ted was stunned. "Cool." That was the best he could do.

After another silence, Ronnie spoke again. "Maybe you and me could party later on. What do you say to that?"

He frowned and leaned his head to the side in suspicion. "You and me?"

Ronnie bit her lower lip seductively, as if considering that. "You don't waste time, do you, Uncle Ted?"

"Not me." He smiled, finally realizing he was making a connection here. "Life's too short to beat around the bush, honey. You want to come over here for a few drinks when you're done?"

"The drinks sound fine, but we can't stay here. Meet me outside the front door in half an hour. Okay, tiger?"

He nodded slowly, the confusion working its way back across his face. "You're not a girl cop, are you, Lesley? I'm in enough trouble with that shit already."

"Don't worry." She straightened up and gave her smoldering smile. "I'm no cop, and this isn't about money."

At that, Ted's head started bobbing. "Then we're on, huh?"

Kostas was standing with his back to the door when Ronnie walked out shortly before eleven. Although it was almost November and the night was overcast, the temperature was in the low sixties. He stood stiff as a light pole, and when he turned to face her, he ground out his cigarette.

"My car is parked across the street," he said, pointing to Federal Boulevard.

"Calm down, tiger. I don't just hop in cars and drive off with strangers. Let's put it back in first gear and go grab that drink. Get to know each other."

"Where?"

Ronnie ran her middle finger along her upper lip. "How about somewhere out of the way? Do you know Charlie Brown's? The piano bar. It's in the Colburn Hotel. We'll have a couple of drinks there for starters." She finished with a wink.

"A hotel?" His eyes flared and he cleared his throat.

"Grant and 10th."

"I'll follow you there. What are you driving?"

Ronnie casually threw her head to the right. "A red Celica."

"Cool." He turned and headed for Federal without another word.

Ronnie got into her car and moved ahead toward the intersection. Once there, she stopped and turned on her right blinker to head north, toward downtown. She looked to her left and saw the white Volvo coming her way, so she moved out onto Federal. Behind Ted's car, Streeter pulled out in Frank's big black Caddy. He didn't want Kostas to recognize him in his brown Buick. It took the little caravan about twenty minutes to get to Charlie Brown's. Ronnie parked and then waited for Ted to walk her into the place; Streeter stayed in his car.

When they'd settled at a low table near the piano, Ronnie ordered a white wine and Ted a Bud Light and a shot of house brandy. The piano player was off that night, and the place was only about half full. Dark and fairly quiet, with the other customers minding their own business.

"I take it you're not a stockbroker or lawyer," she said after the drinks arrived and the waitress left. "You look like a workingman to me."

Kostas sucked in his stomach and took a whack at throwing his shoulders back. "I run my own business. Always have."

"Oh yeah? What kind of business is that?" She set down her glass and gave him her best just-woke-up-and-want-more look.

Ted gulped at his beer and then pulled a Camel from the pack in his shirt pocket. "I'm in what you might call the recycling game." He lit the cigarette and exhaled dramatically.

Ronnie leaned toward him and gave her shoulders a little wiggle. "Some of the girls at Danny's tell me you're kind of an outlaw." Her voice was low and sincere. "That's very sexy. You know, being a renegade and all. One look at you and I could tell you were the type who likes to make up his own rules as he goes along. You live by your own code and you're strictly your own man." She paused to let that sink in. "What is it that you recycle, Uncle Ted?"

He cocked one eye up and nodded like he'd just figured out the most difficult chess move in history. Kostas liked having women know that he was out there. But he really got off on what was sitting next to him at the table. He could feel himself stirring deep down in his pants, which these days wasn't what you'd really call a regular occurrence. "Anything you can name, really. I tell you, Lesley honey, there's practically nothing made by man that I can't get my hands on and turn around and sell for a decent profit." He looked off for a moment. "I sort of specialize in automobiles. Very expensive automobiles, lately."

"That's really neat. What's been happening lately?" Her eyes widened and her mouth opened in anticipation.

The move took his breath away for a second. Again, he struggled to straighten his shoulders. Then he threw her an I've-seen-things-you-wouldn't-believe look. World-weary and wise. "Actually, I'm involved in something bigger than all get-out at the current moment, Lesley."

Ronnie reached her left hand under the table and set it on his right thigh, about halfway between his knee and his groin. Then she gave him a playful squeeze. "Tell me about it. How *big* is it, really?"

At that, Ted just about passed out. He picked up his shot glass and drained it in one pull. Then he nailed the rest of his beer and cleared his throat before answering. This kind of thing just never happened in real life. Not his real life, anyhow. The woman wasn't a cop, so she must be a pro. At that moment, Ted Kostas would have given his life savings to have her. Even for a few days. "Let's just say, little lady, that by this time Saturday I'll a moved a couple ripe Jaguars and I'll have enough cash in hand to take both of us to the Bahamas for a good long time." He paused and studied her face. "How old are you, Lesley?"

"How old do you want me to be?"

Her repartee went sailing over his head, so he just shrugged.

"Well, sir, I'm old enough to know a good thing when I see it. And I'm old enough to go to the Bahamas with a fascinating man without having to ask my mother for permission." She played with her wineglass. "You serious about the trip?"

Ted looked around for the waitress, and when she saw him he waved a callused hand over the table to indicate another round. Looking back at Ronnie, he said, "That's damn straight, little lady."

Ronnie smiled and took another sip of wine. When she finished, she made a production of running her tongue around her lips. "Are you a real outlaw, Uncle Teddy?"

"You might say."

"And how bad are you? Really."

"Bad as I have to be," he responded.

This time Ronnie leaned in and gave him a long look at the cleavage struggling against her top. "Well, do you have bad friends?"

"You might say that I know some heavy people in this here town." He felt himself warming to the topic of his work. "The guy setting up my Saturday deal, he's no one you'd wanna fuck with." He nodded, all serious. "Mitch's been around a little and he's lining me up with a couple of sellers that know the score, too." He paused. "Really heavy people, I'm told."

"Maybe I should be meeting this Mitch guy if he's the one setting it up." Ronnie raised her eyebrows and giggled.

Ted kept quiet for a moment. "Don't you worry about him. He's going to become a regular citizen soon, from what he tells me. I think these cars Saturday are his last move before he takes a real job." He paused. "Listen, I probably said too much here, Lesley, but all you gotta know is that I'm the kinda guy can deliver on what I say. And I'm the kind who can make it worth your while. Don't worry about any of my business associates. *I'm* the man. What say we go back to my place and really party? I live just the other side of Big Danny's. You name your price. I'm sure you're worth it."

"I don't know about this, Uncle Teddy," she said as she withdrew her hand. "It sounds tempting, no doubt about that. But your place?"

Suddenly, Ted's face darkened. "You're not just some teaser, are you?"

Now Ronnie leaned back and studied Kostas. He was done talking. "Of course not. It's just that I don't think I can wait until we get all the way back to that part of town." She threw her head to the side, toward the large doors that opened from the bar to the hotel. "Why don't we just get a room here? That way we can be alone all that much sooner." Her voice was cooking when she'd finished. "And don't worry about the money. You catch the room, the rest is for fun."

Ted broke into a grin so wide it looked about to cut into his filthy beard. "Now you're talking." Then he frowned and looked around. "We'll get those drinks to go up with us, but first I gotta piss like a racehorse." He stood up. "There's gotta be a can up near the hotel desk."

"Go for it," Ronnie said. "A man has to do what a man has to do."

"I'll go whiz and then get us a room," Ted said, his eyes still fixed on the big doors. "When she comes back, see if you can get her to sell us a bottle of something to take up with us."

"You got it, Uncle Ted."

He glanced back down at her one more time, winked and nodded, and then headed for the lobby. By the time he got through the double doors, Ronnie was on her feet. She pulled a tenspot from her purse and walked up to their waitress. "Here's a little something for you," she told the woman as she handed her the money. "Do me a favor? When Grizzly Moron gets back and starts asking for me, just say you think you saw me go into the little girls' room, okay?"

The woman nodded as she pocketed the ten. Ronnie was out the side door and into her car before Ted even finished in the bathroom. She figured she'd be halfway back to the church by the time the poor slob found out that the Colburn only rented rooms by the month. And she'd be almost to Frank's office before Ted gave up waiting for her to come out of the bathroom. She moved out into traffic and in her rearview mirror she could see Streeter following her as she rolled north.

25

"Seems to me you did one hell of an acting job tonight, Miss Ronnie," Frank was saying. "If you could get that old creep to open up, you did a good piece of work."

"Who said I was acting?" Ronnie came back. "I mean, how's a girl supposed to refuse a charmer like Ted Kostas? His aroma alone left me breathless."

The two of them and Streeter were in Frank's office at the church just after midnight. The bondsman swirled a Scotch on the rocks and glanced at his partner, then turned back to Ronnie. "I got a real kick out of watching you in action over at Big Danny's." He shook his head. "You should have seen her, Street. This woman's dangerous."

Streeter took a sip from his Johnnie Walker Red and studied Ronnie. Most of her makeup was worn or wiped off by now. Her hair was calming down, too, and he could see that her skin didn't need any help shining. "That's for sure. I saw enough just from outside. Please tell me you didn't have that outfit in your closet before you got this assignment."

Ronnie casually nursed a Diet Coke and flashed him a quick grin.

"So what exactly did Mr. Kostas have to say?" Frank asked.

"First of all, he's got a big move coming up with Mitch," Ronnie said, setting her Coke down. "He mentioned Mitch specifically. He said that Mitch is setting him up with a couple of people who are going to get him—how'd he say it?—something like 'mint Jaguars.' 'Ripe' was the word I think he used. The point he was struggling to make is that Mitch is lining him up to buy a couple of stolen Jaguars and he's going to turn around and sell them for a huge profit."

"That might be what Bosco's working on with the cops," Streeter said. "He'll probably set up the sale and then have the cops nearby so they can roll in and make the bust." He leaned toward her. "According to those court records you got on Mitch, he's facing a couple of gun-sale charges. This is probably his way of getting his butt off the hook—giving up Kostas. Did he give you any idea when this is happening?"

She nodded. "He said by this time Saturday he's going to have a big chunk of money. I assume that means that the deal will happen Saturday."

Street considered that for a moment. "Or at least be done with by then. First he has to buy the cars. Then he has to sell them. Two separate transactions. He might get the Jaguars tomorrow and store them until he sells them on Saturday. If the cops make their move, it could be at either end, him buying them or him selling them. But I think it would be more likely that they'd do it on the first sale. When Teddy boy buys from the thieves. That's who the cops would want most."

"True enough," Frank interjected. "But it's also possible

that the police are doing the selling. They might have a sting set up for Kostas. Longtime fence like this Greek, they'd have probable cause to set something like that up. And if that's the case, they'd almost certainly come down on him when he's selling the cars. On Saturday. That would be their best time."

"Either way, Teddy's not likely to buy the cars until right before Saturday," Streeter said. "I'm sure he doesn't want them sitting around his place for a couple of days. He'll probably arrange for both transactions to happen on the same day."

"Which leaves us with what?" Ronnie asked. "In terms of Al Lucci, I mean."

"I'm not sure, but Mitch probably feels safe as long as this sting is pending," Frank said, "protected from the cops a little."

"Right," Streeter agreed. "Which might mean that, if he's going after Al again, he'll be inclined to do it on or before Saturday."

"If that's the case," Frank said, "then after Saturday we'll only have to worry about Freddy Disanto."

"I don't know how reassuring that is," Streeter said. "Freddy's already killed one person that we know of. He's still a handful all by himself."

"True, but so far he's used Mitch in dealing with old Al," Frank noted. "At least, as far as we know."

"There was one other thing that Uncle Ted told me," Ronnie said. "He was talking about how this is going to be Mitch's last move like this. Illegal, is what I gather he meant. He said something about Mitch taking a legitimate job after this Jaguar business is done."

"That has to be pure baloney," Frank said. "Guy like Bosco, it's not likely that he'll go on the straight and narrow."

"Not without a major incentive," Streeter concluded.

"And what could that be?" Ronnie asked.

Both men looked at her. Finally, Streeter responded. "I have no idea, and to be honest, I doubt if it matters to us. The thing that concerns me most is keeping Al healthy through the weekend. Not that he'll be out of the woods then, for sure." He paused and smiled. "One thing we have going for us is that we're dealing with people who live in a world where everyone thinks they're smarter than they actually are. And they can almost pull it off, because, with all of them thinking like that, it sort of evens out."

"Why don't you just stay at Lucci's place yourself for the next couple of days?" Frank asked.

"Not a bad idea," his partner said. "I'll call Al first thing in the morning and ask him about that."

Ronnie yawned and stood up. "I'll let you menfolk wrestle with this for now. I'm bushed and I want to slip into something designed for humans. Like my bed." She glanced at Streeter. "Did you have any luck getting ahold of Macmillan down in Arizona today?"

He shook his head. "His secretary said he wasn't available, so I gave him my name and number. Haven't heard back yet. I'll call again tomorrow."

"Good night, gentlemen," she said as she moved toward the door.

"Have a pleasant night's sleep there, Miss Ronnie," Frank said. "You did real good tonight."

"Yeah," Streeter said. "Seeing as how it's almost twelve-thirty, you can come in fifteen minutes later than usual tomorrow."

She looked back at him. "You're insufferable, do you know that?"

He shrugged. "You can make it an extra half-hour if you wear that same little getup again."

"In your dreams, Street. Which seems to be where most of your action is lately."

"That's no way to talk to your boss." He frowned and looked her up and down. "Besides, other than Ted Kostas, I don't see you setting any nights on fire."

"Just don't you worry about me on that score." She nodded. "Good night, all."

When he finished his drink with Frank, the bounty hunter went up to his loft. He was too wired to go right to sleep, so he practiced his piano for nearly an hour. Finally, he started getting ready for bed. Studying his face with a toothbrush sticking out of his mouth, Streeter thought about what Bosco might be up to after the Jaguar sale. Was Kostas serious when he told Ronnie that this would be Mitch's last move before going legitimate? Would Freddy still work on old man Lucci without Bosco? Rinsing out his mouth, Streeter decided he'd worry about all that after he slept.

Before he left the mirror, he leaned forward and studied his hairline. There was a half-full bottle of minoxidil in his medicine chest, and he debated whether to put some on his scalp. That would be a chore. The liquid burned slightly and tended to roll down his face when he applied it. The directions said he must use it twice a day, *every* day, or it wouldn't do any good. He'd been doing just that for about two weeks now, and he didn't see any evidence of its working. Still, the directions specifically stated that he shouldn't expect any growth for at least four months. Streeter shrugged and turned out the light. Walking to his room, he thought how Ronnie was right about him not having any romance going on in his life. You didn't need a thick head of hair to be alone.

26

"Todd, I know you're really up for coming over here, but I'm exhausted tonight," Karen said into the receiver as she studied the middle finger of her left hand. She dabbed some blood-red polish on it and shook the hand lightly while blowing on it. Her eyes rolled slightly as she listened to Todd Janek on the other end of the line.

"It's been three days and I'm starting to back up, if you know what I mean, Karen," he was saying. "Besides, you'll be glad once I get there."

She considered that, knowing he was right. My God, she thought. He puts more effort and energy into the bedroom than into his job, and that hardly seems possible. "You might have a point, but tonight is simply not going to happen. Really, I'm beat. I had three hearings today and I have to be in court in the morning."

"First thing?"

She hesitated. "Not right away."

"Okay, then." He sounded fresh and eager.

No one said anything for a moment. In the silence, Karen recalled how they'd started their affair. She also recalled having second thoughts about it immediately. Well, after the fourth time, at least. Too many Margaritas after they'd finished work Friday night. My oh my, but that man did have a nice little body on him. All she wanted was a little recreational release and they ended up spending most of the weekend together. And Monday night.

"Okay, then, what?" she asked, and frowned as she set down the bottle of nail polish, concentrating fully on the call for the first time. "What we have is nice, Todd, but office romances can be killers."

"That's one way to look at it." He shifted the receiver into his other hand. "Another way is that too much office work can ruin a good sex life."

He knew her career was one of Karen's big priorities, but, hell, he'd performed like a trained monkey when they were together and was always ready for more. Three, four times in—what?—two and a half hours, tops.

"I know we don't *have* to get together tonight, but I thought you might like to," he said. "You're pretty special to me, Karen."

She wasn't sure if he meant it, but it was nice to hear. "Let's hope so." Then she focused on the nail of her left pinkie. "After some of the things we did to each other over the last week, let's just hope so. But this isn't high school. It's the real world, Todd. You're a nice guy and a top-flight investigator. You have my greatest respect in that department. Now, do us both a favor and let's take it a little slower. Okay?"

Todd pulled the receiver from his ear for a moment and

stared at it. He decided to back off and come at it from another direction. "We can talk about Mr. Kostas, too. I've got everything hooked up for tomorrow."

Karen's eyes widened for a second. "Really?"

"Yes ma'am." His voice raised slightly. "First thing right after lunch I go pick up the Jaguar from the dealer. You should see that beast. Maybe about five thousand miles on it and it looks brand-new. Must go for sixty-five out of the showroom. Not a scratch on her, either. Midnight-blue."

Karen debated whether to rework the nail on her pinkie finger but decided against it and set the bottle down. "When do you meet Mitch Bosco?"

Todd rolled his eyes at the name. He couldn't stand Mitch the Snitch, as he referred to him.

"I told him I'd swing by and get him at about one-thirty," Todd responded. "Then we go down to Kostas's place and have him check out the Jag, which should be a piece of cake. If the old Greek knows jack about cars, he'll snap this one up, no questions asked. I figure we'll dick around with him for a couple of hours and then set up the sale for the next afternoon. We'll shoot for noon on Saturday. I want to find out who his buyers are and when they'll be showing up. Where he's going to make that sale, too. Bosco told me that Kostas is unloading them shortly after we make the sale."

Karen frowned, again looking at her nails. "Don't press him too hard on who he's selling to. If we come out of this with just Kostas, I'll be happy. Getting his buyers is a bonus, but not essential. The thing you don't want to do is ask a lot of dumb questions and scare Kostas off tomorrow."

"First place, Karen," he came back with a little bite in his tone, "I don't ask dumb questions, ever. Second place, when this boob sees the quality of the product, he won't care about anything else. We've got him for sure, so why not try and widen the net." He paused. "You trust me, don't you?"

She thought about that for a long moment. "What *choice* do I have at this late date?"

Todd hated it when she used that tone with him. Like he was some student intern she was barely tolerating. "That's about right. I only hope we can trust Mitch the Snitch to hold up his end and sell Kostas on me."

"I've been thinking about that, too," Karen responded. "Before you take him over to that junkyard, Todd, you remind him that, if anything goes wrong with this sting, anything at all, he doesn't get squat from us on Monday at his sentencing. I'll be asking for the max, in fact." She picked up her nail polish again, the receiver cradled in her neck, and pulled out the applicator. "I just wish there was some way we could take both of them down. I hate the idea of Bosco not having to go to jail for anything."

"I wouldn't worry about that, Karen," he said. "A goof like Mitch won't go for very long without screwing up again. I'm sure we'll be seeing his sorry ass back in the system in no time. Karen, how much good do you think this is going to do us with the big guy?"

Karen considered that. "I'm not so sure anymore. When I first talked to the DA about this, I thought we'd be nailing someone major. But the more I know about Ted Kostas, the less impressed I am. Ditto for the boss. Let's put it this way, Todd: We're at a point here where, if this goes off flawlessly as planned, then we go up a small notch in esteem with the DA. If it goes down the toilet, we slip about three notches."

"That sounds great." His voice was flat.

"I wish I could be more optimistic, but we stand to lose more than we can gain, depending on how it comes off. That's why we have to nail Ted Kostas on Saturday. Don't be too concerned with who he's selling to." When she finished speaking, Karen nodded once as she brushed the polish on another nail.

No one spoke for a long time.

"So. Half an hour sound good?" Todd finally asked. Actually, between her reluctance and all the shop talk, he was losing interest in the visit.

"Well, we already discussed the sting."

"Then we can concentrate on the other part."

Karen looked away from her nails. "Give me forty-five minutes, and don't plan on spending the night."

Todd didn't say anything for a long time. "Maybe you're right. Maybe tonight isn't meant to happen."

"Whatever you think is best, Todd. Just make sure and stop by my office when you're through with Ted Kostas tomorrow."

27.

"I'm thinking that, after my little discussion with the D. earlier this afternoon, we're out of the woods with all this nonsense here, Streeter." The old man winced as his stomach recoiled from a gas pain. His entire digestive system—never the best, even during serene times—had been acting up over the last week.

"You mean to tell me that Freddy Disanto is no longer interested in your property?" Streeter looked back from across the Cheese Man's desk late that Thursday afternoon in disbelief. He was filling Al in on what they'd learned from Ted Kostas the night before when the little man sprung the news about Freddy the D. on him. "Just like that? All the trouble he's gone to, all the work and money he put into this deal, and now, poof, it's magically over."

Alphonse Lucci frowned at that and felt another jolt in his lower intestines. "What's so hard to believe? Deals go south all the time, and him not getting my pizza joint made this one too much trouble for Disanto's backers. Let's not look a gift horse in the mouth here, okay?" Al thought back on the entire situation for a moment. "I tell you, I'm just going to enjoy this bit of good news. I don't know how much more of the other kind I can take. I'm sleeping for shit at night, and I'm so wound up, well, I won't even tell you what comes outta me when I go to the john lately. And I miss Maria so much that I'm not too sure right about now if I care whether I'm dead or alive. It's about time this thing ends, big guy." He paused. "I'm not saying I don't appreciate your concern or all the trouble you been through. All I'm saying is that it's over. Let bygones be bygones and all that kind of stuff."

Streeter sat back and thought about it for a moment. "Exactly what did he say the people in Arizona told him?"

Little Alphonse shrugged. "The D. didn't go into what you might call a great amount of detail over it. And I didn't ask for much. About all he said was 'I'm taking my offer off the table. I'm not interested in acquiring the Garlic Bulb no more.' Words along those lines. Me, I'm sitting on the other end of the line half doing cartwheels." He paused, smiling broadly. "Then he goes on to say that his financial backing got tired of the delay in getting the Bulb and that he is no longer connected with them in any professional capacity. Said something about them severing his management contract and buying out his end, which I gather wasn't all that big of an investment on the D.'s part." Al leaned toward his desk and Streeter. "Apparently, Disanto was more the front man in this thing. That's my hunch now. It surprises me somewhat, but that's how it is. Bottom line, Freddy's off my case and the Bulb is no longer in play."

"That doesn't make any sense." Streeter shifted in his seat. "What are they going to do with what they've bought up already? They didn't get those other properties over there for free, you know."

"Course they didn't. The D. says he figures they'll just sell them all individually on the open market. They've had some of those places for over a year, and with property values on the West Side going up the way they are, they'll make out okay. Anything they sell at a loss, well, that's a tax write-off. You know how these big financial types operate, Streeter. They always got a angle. They'll land on their feet. To tell the truth, it sounded to me like the Arizona boys got tired of Freddy's bullshit. Can you blame them? I'd take a write-off myself if it meant not having to deal with him on a regular basis."

"So now what?" Streeter sat back slightly. "You going to bring Maria back?"

"I've got a call in to her already." Al stood up and began pacing slowly behind his desk. "We call off the dogs. That means your services should no longer be required, Streeter." He paused and looked at him. "Don't worry. You can keep whatever money's left from what I gave you the other night. Hell, Disanto even told me he's not going to be working with that head case Mitch Bosco no more. Said they're parting ways."

"He told you that?"

Al nodded wisely.

"Kostas told Ronnie last night that Mitch is getting some kind of legitimate job."

"There you go." Al waved a finger triumphantly at his guest. "Makes perfect sense. The D. fires Bosco because he no longer needs him to make my life hell, so Bosco gets a real job and everyone's happy as a clam. Sometimes life works out nicely."

Streeter studied the little man for a while. "And what about that card-game robbery? You going to just let that one slide?"

"The hell you gotta dwell on that thing for all the time?" Al frowned and shook his head violently. "Those crazy

Ramirez Boys get a wild hair out their butts, so they come down here to try and score a little easy money. Woulda got away with it, too, if one of the idiots didn't shout out Manny's name. That robbery musta just been a coincidence, it happening then. The D. don't know nothing about it, so it musta just been fate or whatever. Give it a rest, Streeter. No harm, no foul."

"I don't know, Al." Streeter stood up now himself. "This just seems too easy. After all you've been through . . . then, out of the blue, Disanto calls and says forget about it. Just like that. Plus, how would the Ramirez Boys even know about your card game? It's not like you put out an ad for it."

Al moved around from behind his desk and placed a hand on Streeter's shoulder. Actually, about as close as he could come was the big man's chest, but he was shooting for the shoulder. "There's plenty a people around town knew about my poker night. Word got up to Wyoming somehow. It's not like we were a secret society or anything like that." He lowered his tone. "Look, I appreciate all you done, Streeter. But your job's over. Take the day off."

Streeter stared at him for a moment and then nodded. "Have you talked to Sheri about this yet?"

The old man shook his head. "I plan on talking to her when I call Maria later. She'll be delighted. My bet is that she comes home with Maria in the next day or two. Life'll get back to normal and Nicky'll get his head screwed on straight. Not a bad outcome." He looked off for a moment. "Sheri's been in on this deal for the Garlic Bulb from day one. Even met with Disanto and me a couple of times. You know, she made some noise all along like she'd be willing to sell the place." He nodded once in triumph. "Guess this shows her I was right about the whole thing. The old man still knows what's what."

"I hope so," Streeter said. He shook Al's hand silently and left the office.

28

Mitch didn't know how to react to the news of Freddy's pulling out of the West Side development deal. The hell is that all about? he thought as he nursed a shot of ginger schnapps at the Satire Lounge on East Colfax Avenue shortly before five that Thursday afternoon. He took a quick pull from his Salem 100 and studied the D., who stood next to him at the bar.

"I'm telling it to you like they told it to me," Disanto was saying without looking directly at Mitch. "That little fucker Niles what's-his-name calls me this morning and tells me they're pulling out. They've got, how did he say it, 'We've got enough on our plate without worrying any further about some little old man who doesn't want to do business with us.' Tells me this thing has dragged out way too long and they're already looking for buyers for the rest of the places over there. Get out from under."

Freddy looked to Mitch unusually pale and incredibly

pissed. Not like he was just making up a story. And why would he? This was not good news. If the development project was finished, obviously there went Bosco's shot at managing it. Mitch waited to see if the D. had more to say. When he didn't, Mitch stepped in. "That doesn't mean you can't go ahead on your own, does it? You got money in that project. Why not just buy them out and keep going on your own?"

Disanto looked at him like he'd just spit up on his shirt. "Using what for money? You got no idea how much these guys put into this thing. Millions. Where the hell am I going to put my hands on that kind of dough?" He shook his head sadly and turned away. "Besides, now I don't have to work with that little pecker Lucci no more. The Arizona guys are giving me back my investment—with a little extra for my efforts—and telling me to be happy. Which is what I intend to be."

"You think those Arizona people might have a change of heart?" Mitch drained his schnapps.

"Not likely. They FedExed some papers first thing this morning for me to sign, getting me off the hook on the proj-ect. My lawyer glanced at them and said it releases me from the whole enchilada." He looked away. "No sir, I believe this baby's over. All over. And the Cheese Man beat me." He didn't say anything for a long time, and then he faced Mitch again. "You know the real pisser here? Lucci's daughter, the horny one with the good ass, she liked the idea of selling to me. I should have worked on her all along and skipped the old hump. Sheri would have been the one to do the deal."

"That's a real pisser there all right, Freddy," Mitch agreed solemnly as he motioned to the bartender for another drink. "You say you talked to Lucci already about this?"

The D. nodded. "Just after lunch. Course, he was happy as all get-out. I never heard a man sound so relieved. Going on about how he wants to forget the whole thing and get his life back to normal. Bring his wife back to town and all that good stuff." Freddy paused and studied the man leaning on the bar next to him. "You know, this means I won't be needing your services from now on."

Mitch considered that. "The thought crossed my mind. What about that card-game robbery? You were the one all worked up over that, weren't you?"

Freddy turned to look at the back bar. "True. I still might want to have the guy suffer some for that. But I'll deal with it later. My first job is to find those other two Ramirez Boys and settle up with them. Lucci can wait." Then he faced Mitch again. "How about you? Your deal with the police over yet, or what? Oh, yeah, I know a few people downtown and they told me a little about it. And seeing that look on your face just now, I know they told me right. I hear Kostas is still in business, so I figure you've got some work to do on that count."

"Yeah," Mitch said as casually as he could. "It's coming up soon. Next couple of days. Kostas has his money together, and the cops are really on me to hook them up. Come Saturday, you won't be seeing Ted Kostas around anymore."

"I never see him around now," Freddy said. "It's just that I hear things."

"That doesn't concern you, Freddy," Mitch offered mildly as he picked up his new drink.

"Don't get touchy there, Mitchie. I'm just making conversation, is all." Freddy straightened up from the bar and laid two tens on it. "I probably won't be seeing you for a good long time." He waited a beat. "Maybe never again. It's been weird knowing you. Take care, Mitchie."

I'll just do that little thing, Mitch thought as he watched the D. walk out of the room and into the darkening outside world. Now what? All his plans for working with Niles and the Arizona people were going up in smoke. No calls from Niles in days, and now they were pulling out of the project, leaving Mitch with squat and a few empty promises. He glared at the shot glass in his hand, and then he tilted back his head and drained the schnapps. When he'd put the glass down, he decided to go home and think about a new plan.

By the time Mitch drove the ten minutes back to his apartment building, he knew that he had one last chance to salvage a job from the Arizona people. His first concern was getting a hold of them, so he was very relieved when he checked his phone-message machine and heard Niles's voice.

"There has been a sudden change in plans, Mr. Bosco," Niles said. "Mr. Disanto is no longer involved in the project, and we've decided to take a different approach. Please call me at your earliest convenience to discuss how you might fit in with that." He concluded by leaving a pager number.

Mitch quickly punched in the digits, and while he was waiting for the return call, he pulled out his "Prosperity Journal" and wrote out some thoughts. "The key to most success is taking adversity and turning it into opportunity. I'm faced with a golden one right now. Disanto is history, the old man is vulnerable, and I'm motivated to do what it takes. And I mean *whatever* it takes. Must convince Niles to seize the moment. Must convince him that—"

Just then the phone rang. Mitch set the journal on his coffee table and crushed out his cigarette. "Yes?"

"Mr. Bosco. Niles here." The voice betrayed nothing.

"Yeah, Niles." Mitch struggled to keep his voice even. "I'm glad you called. I just got done meeting with Freddy Disanto."

"Oh? And did he speak of the development project?"

"That he did. He tells me it's stillborn. You guys are

pulling out and he's no longer involved at all." Mitch cleared his throat. "That puts me out of work, so, when I got your call, it started me thinking."

Nothing from the other line at first, and then, "And what did you decide?"

"I decided that this deal could still be made if Al Lucci was out of the picture. His daughter, Sheri, she'd take a decent offer if she was in control of the restaurant, which she would be if old Al weren't around."

"That's an amazing coincidence, Mr. Bosco," Niles said with more life. "We were thinking much the same thing down here. But our first concern was terminating our relationship with Mr. Freddy Disanto. He was useless. Not really a bottom-line kind of man. Plus, he was difficult to control. Impossible, in fact. The story we told him today was merely to get rid of him. Which leaves only the problem of taking Mr. Lucci out of the equation."

Mitch cleared his throat again and gulped to get more air. "That wouldn't be hard to do. That equation business."

"What are you proposing?"

"Well, sir, the D. was farting around, trying to scare Lucci to his senses. I'd come at it from a more direct line. I think Lucci was scared half to death for a while there. I propose that we make him totally dead. And now would be a particularly good time, seeing as how he has to be feeling pretty safe, what with the D. telling him the project is over."

Niles was silent for a long time. "What would you expect if you were to take care of Mr. Lucci?"

"Just what we've been talking about. Cash up front—twenty-five thousand—and a permanent job as your man in Denver. Project supervisor or manager or whatever you want to call it." He paused. "At a healthy rate of pay."

"How quickly could you move on this?" Niles asked softly.

"Right away. You get me something in writing about the job, and Mr. Lucci will be taken care of within twenty-four hours."

"That soon?" Niles waited a moment before continuing. "I'll overnight you an employment agreement on the management position. If it's all right with you, sign it and return it to me. When the Lucci matter is completed, I'll sign from this end. You'll also be receiving half the cash as down payment. The other half will come when Mr. Lucci is no longer a problem. Does that sound fair enough?"

Mitch thought it sounded more than fair. He nodded to his kitchen and then he spoke into the phone. "That should do her."

"Excellent, Mr. Bosco. Obviously, discretion is absolutely essential. You will be working alone, won't you?"

"Sure will. This here's a one-man job." Then Mitch thought of another item. "What if Freddy Disanto hears about it and gets his nose out of joint? Comes after me or goes to the cops? You give that any thought?"

"Yes, we have," Niles said confidently. "We've compensated Mr. Disanto in the event that we decide to proceed with the development project at some future date."

"If you say so." With that, they both hung up.

Mitch lit another cigarette and looked back at his journal. He scratched out the incomplete line he had begun before Niles called and continued to write. "Niles is one step ahead of me. We've arranged for me to take Al Lucci out of the game and then I get the goodies." He thought before he wrote the next sentences. "I'll do it Saturday around noon. Just as the police are doing a number on T.K. Saturday night should be one major celebration. The fruits of planning for success."

29.

From the moment they met, Todd Janek and Ted Kostas disliked each other. Todd thought Kostas looked like a disgusting old pervert, while Kostas figured Todd for some kind of scrawny San Fransisco fairy. Luckily, they were both able to agree right off the bat that they could do business together. It was the Jaguar—shiny, gorgeous, midnight-blue—that brought them together. Kostas practically went rigid with greed when he saw Todd and Mitch pull into his lot shortly after lunch on Friday.

"Holy smokes," he bellowed as he walked out of the shack, wiping idly at the French-fry remnants clinging to his beard. "The other one in this good a shape?" he asked Mitch, who nodded. "Then I do believe we can come to terms here and now." He leaned in the driver's window and let out a whistle of approval when he read the odometer. "Less than seven thousand miles." He pulled his head out and shot Todd a hard frown. "Them honest miles on there, *sonny boy?*"

"That they are, *pops,*" Todd came back. He knew he should try and get along with the fat man, but he couldn't resist giving him grief.

The two men stood a few feet apart, savoring the bad vibes. Observing the sour chemistry, Mitch stepped in.

"Okay, fellas," he said soothingly. "No need for name-calling here. Right? I mean, we're all on the same team, basically. Just play nice and everyone gets to go home rich." He looked at each of the men individually. "Ted, Todd. Todd, Ted."

They grunted in unison, and then Kostas turned to the car. Shined up like she was ready for a contest, the motor running so quietly you practically couldn't hear it unless you popped the hood. He figured, fully loaded like it was, this baby would go for close to eighty thousand brand-new. Then and there, he knew he'd be asking thirty-seven five for each of them the next day. More than double his money for a couple of hours of work. His buyers were solid, and he wouldn't be keeping the Jags for more than two hours. Three, tops. He'd worked with Mitch before, so this figured to be a no-risk no-brainer.

As he flashed on Lesley from Big Danny's, a quick wave of regret swept over him. Lesley my ass, he thought. What she had been up to, Kostas couldn't begin to fathom. But he'd gone back to Danny's the morning after he met her and got some degree of satisfaction when Danny said he'd just fired her for skimming. By now, standing here next to the mint Jag in the cool autumn wind, he didn't care all that much anymore. He'd buy himself some other little plaything for his celebration the next night.

Dressed in a black leather biker jacket and tight blue

jeans, Todd slowly stepped toward the Greek and extended his hand. "Didn't mean anything by that 'pops' crack." He forced a smile as he eased himself upwind of Kostas. The man smelled like two months' worth of foul laundry.

For his part, Ted glanced over at the hand and just nodded. Then he said to Mitch, "I'll want a test run." He paused. "Just you and me."

"Hop in, pal," Mitch said without hesitation. "I'll ride shotgun."

Ted backed the car carefully down the short, wide driveway and onto the street. But once he got there, he couldn't resist ramming it into first gear and letting the clutch fly out as he leaned into the gas pedal. The resulting squeal of tires, burning rubber, and quick fishtail to each side with the rear end made Todd wince in agony as he watched. "Stupid Jagoff," the investigator mumbled to himself as he zipped up his jacket. When the car was out of sight, he did a quick walking inventory of the yard. Then he went to the street and studied the layout of the neighborhood.

Mitch sat in the passenger's seat, a weak smile plastered on his face, watching Kostas work his way through the gears to third. "I don't think you want to bang her up out here right about now, Ted," he said softly to the driver. "Car won't be worth shit if it's all smashed in."

Kostas frowned but laid off the gas pedal and eased the car back into second. "True enough." Then he shot Mitch a glance. "What do you know about this Todd guy? You ask me, I'd say he looks like a queer or a fed or something like that. How come I never heard of him?"

Mitch shrugged. "All I know is he's got two of these things and he wants to unload them fast. He says the thirty you're offering'll work just fine. What else do you need to know? I did some business with him a few years ago and it went all right." Then he leaned toward the driver slightly. "Besides, there's lots of people you never heard of that are still good people."

Ted considered that for a couple of blocks and then headed the Jag back toward his lot. "Then why aren't you gonna be there tomorrow when we make the deal?" he finally asked.

"Like I told you, I'm just getting a finder's fee for this thing." Mitch tried to keep his voice patient. "I'm getting out of all this outlaw stuff, Ted. From now on, it's strictly aboveboard employment for me. I get ten percent of the sale price for hooking you up with the man. For that little, you two can make the transaction yourselves."

"Who's he bringing to drive the other one?"

"His brother. Ed."

"I might want to check them out," Ted said as he turned up the street leading to T.K. Scrap. "These two guys got a last name?"

"I'm sure they do." Clearly, Mitch was becoming bored.

When Mitch didn't elaborate for more than a block, Ted turned to him. "So what is it? The last name, I mean."

"I don't know and I don't care." Mitch turned in his seat, the better to face Ted. "And you know there's no way in hell you're going to check them out. Listen, this is one sweet deal for you. Don't blow it by asking a lot of questions. I say these brothers are stand-up guys. Just do the deal and count your money." Then he smiled. "You know I wouldn't put you in a bad place here, Ted, don't you? What's the worst thing can happen? They don't show up. You're not out nothing."

Ted looked sternly through the windshield and finally nodded. He pulled the dark Jaguar slowly into the lot and shut off the engine. By this time, Todd Janek was standing near the dog pen next to the main shack, watching Ted's Dobermans. They reflected their owner: both were fairly fat for their breed, slow-moving, and without expression most of the time. When he saw the car roll into the lot, he headed in that direction. As the men got out of the Jaguar, Todd took his best shot at a sincere smile. He didn't miss by much.

"Is that a dream or what?" he asked Kostas, who was opening the hood by the time he got to him. "I must be a lunatic, letting them go for that price."

Ted glanced over at him and nodded. "You'll make a buck." With that he turned his attention back to the engine.

For his part, Mitch Bosco was lighting a Salem 100 and shivering slightly in his white windbreaker. The clouds were coming in from the west, and the temperature must have dropped to the mid-forties by now. Mitch looked over at Todd and, when he caught his eye, flashed him a quick grin and gave him a solid thumbs-up with his left hand. Todd nodded but said nothing.

Finally, Ted moved his upper body out from under the hood and shut it carefully. He looked directly at Todd when he spoke. "You say the other one is just as good."

"Easily," Todd answered. "Deep forest-green and only sixty-one hundred miles on her. Every bit as loaded, too."

"And you can get them here by noon?" He paused. "Make it twelve-thirty tomorrow. My buyers'll be coming a little after that, so I'll need them by twelve-thirty. You can do that?"

Todd nodded several times, his smile broadening.

"It'll be just you and your brother, right?"

Another series of nods.

Ted considered that and glanced at his dog pen. "Here's how it'll work. You guys pull up and get out of the cars. Then you lay down the keys and paperwork over on the office stoop." He tossed his head in that general direction. "I'll be inside, but the money will be in a suitcase with the dogs. Now, your brother turns around and leaves the yard and keeps on walking. I don't want to see him no more. Then you go in the pen by yourself and get the money. It'll be wide open. Try any funny stuff and I give the Dobermans there the attack command." He frowned for emphasis. "You behave yourself and everything's fine. Just grab the suitcase and walk on out of here. When you get to the front gate, shut it and put on the padlock. Then just keep walking and we never see each other again. Think you can handle that?"

"You've got it, partner," Todd said. "When do the buyers show up?"

Ted's frown deepened and he looked hard at Mitch. "What the fuck is this, Bosco? A quiz show?" He glanced back at Todd. "What the hell you care about the buyers for?"

"Forget about it." Todd innocently held his hands up, palms toward Ted. "None of my business, right?"

"Damned straight, it ain't."

Todd now extended his hand to be shaken. "Then we have us a deal. Thirty thousand for the two hot Jags. Cash. We'll be here at twelve-thirty tomorrow."

Kostas looked down at the hand for a couple of seconds, grunted something that sounded inhuman, nodded, and walked toward the office.

As Todd backed the Jaguar out of the lot, he was happy. Although he hadn't gotten much on the wire he was wearing, he was sure that the buyers would show up at T.K. Scrap within an hour or so of his selling the cars to Kostas. Maybe sooner than that. Which meant he and Karen would have an unmarked car and a team of detectives waiting at the end of the block to nail both Kostas and his customers. Not a bad day's work. As he headed toward the freeway, his thoughts drifted to the dinner he had planned for that night with

Karen. And to going back to her place later. Nothing more to be done today about Mr. Ted Kostas.

Mitch glanced at Todd from time to time, thinking what a boneheaded move it was for him to press the Greek about the time the buyers would show up. Lucky for the DA's investigator they were dealing with Kostas. Anyone with something close to a brain between their ears would have smelled the cop's question and probably called the whole deal off. But who cares now? Mitch thought. He'd done his part, and by this time tomorrow, Ted would be heading downtown with the police. That reminded him what he had planned for Al Lucci at about the same time. Yes sir, Saturday was going to be one hell of a life-altering day.

That morning, Mitch had read and signed the papers from Arizona. Mailed them back before Todd the Clod picked him up in the Jag. In another twenty-six hours, give or take, Mitch's debt to the law would be paid and Alphonse Lucci would be dead. And by about this time Monday, he'd get the second half of the payment from Arizona and his probation would be a done deal. Then he'd start his new life in corporate management. He couldn't wait for Todd to drop him off so he could write about it in his "Prosperity Journal." That and hoist a few victory ginger-schnappses.

30

Ted Kostas stared at Freddy Disanto's forearms—because they were bigger than any he had ever seen before, and because he was afraid to look directly into the D.'s eyes. You couldn't really blame him for that. Not with the D. sitting there glaring at him like he'd just stomped on his shoes. Ted would have to be a total idiot not to be mildly concerned, at the very least. The D. was out of Ted's league and he knew his best move now was to shut up, be respectful, and hear the man out. About his only move, in fact. The two men were sitting in the basement of one of Disanto's restaurants, the D. having summoned Kostas with a phone call a couple of hours after Mitch and Todd left his scrap yard.

"I'm afraid you've gotten yourself into a situation here, and I do believe that I might have a way to help you out of it," Freddy was saying. "You have any idea what I'm talking about?"

With great hesitation, Ted nodded and frowned in confusion and fear, his eyes still averted.

"I can't help thinking that you don't." Freddy's voice was low and thick, like he was speaking through a towel. "First of all, I want to hear you say the words. Gestures don't mean nothing to me. And second of all, I like for the people I'm talking to, I like it for them to look right at me when we're having our talk."

Ted's head shot up and he forced himself to make eye contact. "Okay, I got no idea what you're talking about. I admit to that, Mr. Disanto." Kostas had never met Freddy before that day, but he had heard about him: his physical strength and his legendary temper. That he dabbled in the lesser vices and was rumored to have killed a man. You don't screw around with the D., is exactly what Ted Kostas had always heard. And seeing the big hairy man up close did nothing to change his mind one bit.

Freddy nodded. "That's better, Ted. Here's the situation I'm referring to. I hear a lot of things about what's going on around town. People tell me about this and that all the time. Now, certain people tell me that this Greek guy named Kostas is making a major purchase in the near future." He studied the man. Ted was wearing filthy coveralls. Balding slightly, chubby, bearded. Probably stubborn in a scared, moronic sense. That was Disanto's read. "They tell me you're buying a couple of mint cars and you've already got people lined up to take them off your hands for a nifty profit. Any of this ring true?"

Ted shifted in his seat and glanced around the room, wondering how Disanto knew about the Jaguars. Not that it mattered at the moment. The basement was damp and poorly lit. It smelled like rotten tomatoes and stale beer, making Ted's stomach feel queasy. He looked back at the D., who was bearing down on him with a stare that could stop a train.

"Who told you?" Ted finally asked. "Bosco? That kid—Todd whatever?"

"It really isn't important, but Mitch Bosco mentioned it," Disanto replied. He took a deep breath and sat back. Ever since Mitch had first mentioned the Jaguar sting, Freddy's mind had been working overtime trying to figure an angle. Some way to get his hands on the cash that Ted Kostas had pulled together for the deal. He had gotten a few details from Mitch, but at the moment the D. was mostly improvising. "The point is you're being set up, Mr. Kostas."

Ted's eyes shot up when he heard that one. "Set up? By who? The cops or what?"

"No, not the police." The D. was smiling slightly now, liking the growing fear he smelled from Kostas. The hook was set. "This seller. Todd, you say his name is? He and his people have no intention of delivering any cars to you. Not permanently, anyway." He paused and flexed the enormous muscles on his forearms. "Exactly when are they supposed to deliver the things?"

"Mitch is in on it?" Ted's fear was turning to anger.

"Now, that's a question there, Ted. No fair, you answering my question with one of your own. The delivery. When and where?"

"Tomorrow, at my place. Around noon." He thought for a moment. "Twelve-thirty."

"And I suppose Mitch vouched for these people."

Ted nodded. "Yeah."

"But he's not going to be there personally, correct?" Though Freddy was winging it here, he was reasonably certain he was on the right track.

"Uh-huh." More nodding.

"Typical of that little shit." Freddy grimaced and then

stood up, leaning his hands on the small table between them. "He makes me want to throw up, you know that? I bet you're none too thrilled with him right about now, either."

"You can take that to the bank," Ted said as he took in a huge sniff of the D.'s aftershave. Some kind of designer smell he'd never encountered before. Looking up at the man leaning in to him now, he guessed that Disanto must go close to two thirty. Ted could feel his mouth getting drier by the minute. "You got anything here for me to drink?"

"Would a beer work?"

"Just about perfect." Ted felt a hint of relaxation for the first time since he'd heard from the D. on the phone.

Freddy walked to a small refrigerator with rounded edges in one corner of the room, opened it, and pulled out a long-necker of Killian's Red. In one smooth motion he twisted off the cap and walked back to where Ted Kostas was sitting. "Enjoy," he said, handing the bottle to him.

"Thanks, Mr. Disanto," Ted said as he grabbed the beer. It felt ice cold, and he drank about a third of it in one long gulp. When he finally came up for air, his eyes watered and his temples ached. "Why did Bosco tell you about all this? I can't see why he'd talk to anyone."

The D. shrugged innocently. "He and me used to be in a sort of business arrangement together. Bosco has a big mouth. He's the kind that tells people things that are really better left unsaid." He leaned back into the table. "The point is, what he said is true. The question then becomes, what are we going to do about it?"

"We?" Ted took another long gulp from his beer, setting his temples to aching once more.

"Precisely." The D.'s eyes darkened and his voice lowered. "I want to help you out on this thing. Arrange it so you can still get those Jags and make your sale. I also wouldn't mind seeing to it that Bosco gets shafted."

Ted frowned and adjusted himself in his chair. "How could you do that?"

"By covering your backside."

"Huh?" The beer was starting to loosen Ted up a little.

"First off, tell me how the deal is supposed to go down."

The D. stood up straight now and began pacing slowly in front of the small table as Ted gave him a quick summary of how he and Todd were to exchange the cars and cash.

"And you're supposed to be inside your office the whole time?" the D. asked when Ted had finished.

"That's right. My plan was to yell to the dogs through the window if Todd and his brother try to pull something." Ted was frowning now, studying Disanto's face closely. "What did Bosco tell you they would do?"

The D. thought about that for a long moment. Then he came up with a line and fed it to Kostas. "The way he told me, when the cars are to arrive at your place, the drivers would go through the motions like you planned. But this Todd guy would take his own sweet time picking up the money. Meanwhile, his brother, or whatever the guy is, will have gone around your yard and come in the back way." He paused and frowned at Ted. "You *do* have a back door to your office, right?"

Ted Kostas nodded. "Comes in right off the alley."

"See, they know that," the D. continued, relieved. "Anyhow, at the time Todd is collecting the suitcase, the other guy is pounding on your door. They figure you'll do one of two things: either open the door, in which case he shoots you; or get distracted by the knocking and all, at which time Todd picks up one set of keys and papers and drives off with a Jag. You don't open the door, the brother goes back, gets the other set of keys, and drives off with the other Jag."

Ted was shaking his head in disbelief by the time he'd finished. "That sounds like the dumbest thing I ever heard of. It musta taken them all of two minutes to come up with that one." He looked off for a bit. "What's to keep me from just calling the dogs to tear Todd apart?"

"If these guys aren't afraid to shoot you, why would they hesitate shooting a couple of mutts?" Disanto asked.

"That makes a lot of noise."

"You ever hear of silencers?"

Ted struggled to find more loopholes in the plan. "Well, what's to stop me from shooting back?"

The D. shrugged dramatically. "Mitch says they don't figure you to be armed, or if you are, you don't have the balls to defend yourself. Plus, they're counting on the element of surprise being heavily in their favor." He paused and gave Ted a sympathetic nod. "To be perfectly honest here, Kostas, they don't give you much credit for brains or guts."

Ted drained his beer in one mighty gulp and then slammed the bottle down on the table. "We'll just see about that." Then he looked back up at the D. "You say you want to cover my backside?"

"You got it. I figure, if I station myself out in the alley, I can head off the one guy. From your end, when Todd gets in the dog pen you can turn the mutts loose." He narrowed his eyes. "You keep any weapons in the office?"

"Sure do. I have a little .22 and I can bring my .38 from home."

The D. smiled. "You do that. You bring everything. The money, the suitcase, the guns. When the dogs hit Todd, you come out waving the .38 and bring him back inside. That gives us both the guys and the cars."

"What happens next?" Ted sat back, his mouth opening slightly.

"You give me the money and keep the cars. I'll take care of the two tough guys." Having said that, the D. sat down across from Ted and smiled.

"You get all the money?" Ted frowned now.

"Of course I do." Disanto's eyes flared. "I just saved your fat ass from getting shot and I arranged it so you keep the cars. Plus, I have to get rid of Todd and his friend. I shouldn't get compensated for that? Give me a break here. If it wasn't for me you'd be dead. Look at it this way: if things went the way you originally planned, you'd be out the thirty thousand anyhow. You'll make out fine."

"What about Mitch? Ain't he gonna come after me when this thing blows up on him?"

The D. hadn't considered that, so he shrugged. "You let me worry about Mitch Bosco." He held out his hand. "We in agreement here?"

Slowly, Ted nodded and stuck his hand out to be shaken. "All right. How will I know when you're back there in the alley?"

"I'll show up at about noon. I'll come to the back door to your office, so leave it open for me. We'll go through everything one more time, and then you show me a good spot to wait out back where I won't be seen. Don't worry, Ted. This thing'll be over before you know it."

Kostas stood up now. "Can I go now?"

The D. nodded. "Just remember to bring the .38 and the cash. We got to make this look realistic." He paused. "And, Ted, try and get a good night's sleep tonight. Like I said, this thing'll be over before you know it."

After he had walked Kostas back to his car outside, the D. went back to the office in the rear of the restaurant. He was still stewing over the Lucci fiasco. That was another matter, but to tell the truth, Disanto was almost glad it had turned out the way it did. He hated the Arizona people, particularly that little schmuck Niles Macmillan. They'd only met a couple of times, but Niles had treated him like an idiot. Just another wimp in a suit. That's how the D. pegged him.

Niles and his associates had given him so many orders in general, and so much crap about not getting Lucci's place, that last week, by the time Niles started hinting at killing the old man, the D. had told him to shove it. He just wanted out of the project, so he picked a fight with Niles over the phone. Within a couple of hours he was offered the buyout. The Arizona people said they'd found someone else who might be able to negotiate with the Lucci family. Niles even went so far as to say it was a Denver man they'd pegged for the job. The D. suspected Mitch Bosco, for Mitch had let it slip once that he had talked to Niles on the phone.

Who the hell can you trust anymore? The D. asked himself as he sat behind his desk. Then he thought about Ted Kostas. Teddy boy would be wondering the same thing long about noon tomorrow, the way the D. had it planned. The thirty thousand in cash would at least compensate Freddy for his grief from the Arizona boys, and the Jaguar sting going all to hell would blow Mitch's plea bargain with the DA's office. There was plenty of justice in all of that. When you can't trust the people around you, the D. reasoned as he sat there, at least you can trust your own wits and take action.

31

Streeter slept for a total of maybe four hours that Friday night. He kept waking up and thinking about old man Lucci. How his problems with Disanto and the Arizona developers had just disappeared too easily. Way too easily. When he finally woke up for good at about six, he decided it was a nice morning to take a drive up to Cheyenne. Maybe tie up at least one loose end while he was at it. The Ramirez Boys and the card-game robbery had nagged at him since he first heard about it. What was that all about? As he dressed in jeans and a hooded sweatshirt, he figured that, if he could find out who put them up to the job, he'd have something to go on. What that would be, he had no idea.

It was shortly before eight when he pulled into downtown Cheyenne. Streeter had always thought the city was fairly flat and nondescript. If he wanted any real flavor of the Old West, he'd take the extra hour and drive to Laramie. But on this morning he wasn't interested in local color. He parked his car downtown and went into a diner near the State Capitol. Then he ordered coffee, grabbed the phone book from behind the counter, and looked up the address and phone number for a Glenda Switt; a newspaper wire story he'd read about Albert Hepp had said that Hepp was visiting her mobile home at the time of his death. Streeter also tried to find anyone with the last name of Hepp and found none. He'd hoped to talk to Albert's surviving relatives. Then he checked out the surname Ramirez and found six of them listed. He wrote down all the numbers and addresses, figuring he'd call them if he struck out with Glenda Switt. When he finished his coffee, he drove to the mobile-home park on the northern edge of the city where she lived.

"What is it?" Glenda asked when she opened the side door a crack. She was tying up her terry-cloth bathrobe and blinking to get her eyes focused.

"I'm looking for Glenda Switt," Streeter said.

"Not anymore, you're not. Now you're looking *at* Glenda Switt." She smiled briefly at that one.

Her grin exposed a mouth that had seen precious few trips to the dentist's office. Streeter immediately counted two missing teeth near the front, and the remaining ones were badly stained from—judging by a breath of astounding range—coffee and cigarettes. Glenda was a redhead, pushing forty and no stranger to groceries. But she had a friendly, open face and kind green eyes.

"My name is Streeter. I'm a private investigator doing research for a gentleman in Denver." He leaned into the doorframe. "Do you know Albert Hepp?"

Glenda's face clouded. "I used to. Al's dead." She looked down.

"Right. I meant 'used to.' " He paused. "Listen, Glenda, I don't want to stir up any bad memories, but we believe that Albert was involved in a robbery down in Denver just before he died. I'm trying to track down the man who set it up. I think it's the same person who's trying to hurt my client."

"You know who shot Al?" Her face brightened for a second.

"I'm not sure." He didn't want to go into Freddy the D. just then. "Did Albert talk about a robbery the day before he died?"

"He said something about a job down in Colorado that day, and then all of a sudden he had a couple of grand the night he was shot. My hunch was that he didn't inherit the money." She retied her robe casually as she spoke and then shrugged. "I never asked him much about his work, and he was a man of few words. Believe me on that one. About all he said was that him and Manny and Neal had a job and that something went wrong, so them other two left town for Canada or Oregon or like that." She looked off for a moment. "I expect that Al should of gone with them, but he was a stubborn one. He was tired of Manny bossing him around, so he stayed here." She cleared her throat. "Al was a sweet man in a lot of ways, but smart thinking never was a strong suit of his."

"Did he ever mention any names regarding who hired them?"

She shook her head. "The way those boys operated, everything came through Manny. Al and Neal couldn't organize a bake sale on their own." She stared closely at Streeter for a while and then took a deep breath. "You might ask Manny's sister. He was staying with her at the time."

"Do you know where she lives?"

"Not exactly."

Streeter pulled the list of Ramirez names and addresses from his pants pocket and read them to her. She stopped him at "L. Ramirez." "That's probably the one. Linda's the sister's name, and I think she lives over on that part of town." She gave him directions, nodded once, and closed the door.

It took Streeter about fifteen minutes to find Linda Ramirez's home. As he pulled up in front of the small wood-frame house, Linda herself was just coming out the door and heading for a small blue car parked in the driveway. She was a tall woman of about thirty, with dark, handsome features and a no-nonsense way about her. She turned that on high the minute Streeter introduced himself and told her what he was after.

"Look, mister," she said as she opened her car, "my brother's long-gone and I don't know where he is. Manny's not the kind to write, either."

"I just wanted to know if you had any idea who he was working for right before he left. I'll be happy with a name. Anything."

She looked up at him intently. "And I should tell you because . . . ?"

Streeter nodded and pulled out his wallet. He took out a fifty and two twenties and handed them to her. "Because why not? Like you said, Manny's long-gone, and you could maybe help me with my little problem. I'm not interested in finding your brother or giving him any hassles. It's the guy who hired him I want to talk to."

She took the bills slowly, studying his face the whole time. "You're not with the law, right?"

Streeter shook his head. "Not even close."

"All I know is that he was talking to someone named Mitch on the phone a night or so before they split. The next thing, Manny and Neal are leaving Wyoming and Albert Hepp ends up dead. That's *all* I know." With that, she got into her car, closed the door, and started the engine.

Streeter walked to his Buick, got in, and headed back to Denver. As he moved south on I-25, he knew he had to find

Alphonse Lucci as soon as he could. If Mitch Bosco had set up the card-game robbery, he was working a weird angle that Streeter couldn't imagine. But it probably didn't involve Freddy the D., which meant that Alphonse might still be in trouble. Crossing the state line into Colorado, he grabbed his cell phone and called the church.

"Frank, I want you to do me a favor."

"Where are you?"

"I'm heading down twenty-five," Streeter said. "I was up in Cheyenne talking to a few people, and I think it was Mitch Bosco who set up that card-game robbery at Lucci's."

"Why would he do that?"

"I have no idea, but it seems to me that something's going on here that we don't know about. Look, Frank, get a hold of old man Lucci. Fast. If he's not at home, call his restaurants. Have him come down to the church right away. If Bosco's freelancing, I'm thinking that he could still come after Al."

Frank considered that for a moment. "Why would he? I thought Al told you that Disanto said they don't want to buy him out anymore."

"That's what he said, but Bosco's the one who has me worried now. Maybe I'm just being paranoid, but I want to talk to Al about it."

"Better safe than sorry, huh? How far away are you?"

"I'll be home in about forty-five minutes."

When Streeter got back to town, he went right to the church. He headed for Frank's office, where he found the bondsman on the phone. Al Lucci was not there. Frank hung up soon after his partner arrived.

"I struck out with your Mr. Lucci," he said. "There was no answer at his house or his restaurants. I talked to someone at his catering shop and they had no idea where he is."

Streeter stood in front of the desk considering that. "Did you leave messages everywhere?"

Frank nodded. "Told them to have him head over here pronto. Or at least call. What do you think Bosco's up to?"

"Probably nothing, but I'll feel better if I know where Al is, not to mention finding out where Mitch Bosco is, too." He paused. "Keep after Al's numbers. Even the catering place. Call me on the cell phone if you hear anything. I'm going over to Bosco's place to see if he's home. I have no idea why he would have arranged that robbery, but I'd sure like to ask him about it."

"You're going to tell him you know?" Frank frowned. "That doesn't sound very smart. Remember, this is the same guy that already threw some shots at your car."

"Which means I'm probably not on his Christmas-card list as it is. What else can he do?"

With that, Streeter turned and headed for the door. He got back into his Buick and drove to Mitch's apartment building. The Volvo station wagon was not in the lot or on the street, but the bounty hunter rang Mitch's apartment number anyhow. Rang it seven times, in fact, and still got no response. Frank hadn't called, so Streeter took a quick spin over to Lucci's house. No one was home. Then he decided to run past both of Alphonse's restaurants to see if he was at either. If that failed, Streeter figured he'd go home and wait to hear from him.

32

As he ate his breakfast that morning, Mitch was absolutely convinced that the last day of Al Lucci's life would be the pivotal day in the rest of his own. His legal troubles would end with the arrest of Ted Kostas and, at about the same time, he would be entering corporate America by killing the Cheese Man. True, when Mitch started his "Prosperity Journal" he'd had no intention of taking a straight job. Not to mention that he had never seriously considered murder before, either. But how was he to know that an opportunity like the one Niles presented would pop up? A man would have to be a damned fool to turn his back on something like that, and Mrs. Bosco sure didn't raise any idiots. When he finished eating, he pulled out his journal and made a quick entry over the last of his coffee and a cigarette.

"As I recall," he began, "one of the Seven Habits of Highly Effective People is that you constantly re-evaluate your progress so that you can make the appropriate adjustments.

Something like that. So today is adjustment day. I never intended to take an actual job, but this is a move that just makes too much sense not to do. Besides, I have a feeling that working for Niles and his company shouldn't be that much different than what I've been doing all along. This development hustle sounds like robbery with retirement benefits, is all. About the only real change is that I'll get to wear a suit. Seventy thousand a year for starters, plus sick pay and whatnot. I have no choice. Not really."

He paused and thought about killing Alphonse Lucci. "Taking out the old man is just another adjustment I have to make," he wrote. "Strictly a one-time deal. A man has to be open to opportunity or he'll never grow. Besides, if I can't extend myself this once, how bad do I want success?" With that question, he carefully closed the book.

After he'd shaved and showered, Mitch slowly dressed himself. Then he checked his nine-millimeter automatic to make sure it was loaded and the safety was on. Not that he planned on shooting Alphonse, but he'd need the small weapon for persuasion purposes. As he put on his coat to leave at exactly eleven-fifteen, the phone rang.

"Yeah?" he asked curtly into the receiver.

"Mitch, my boy," Todd Janek's voice came at him all cheerful. "How's it going?" Without waiting for an answer, he continued. "Got one quick question for you, slick."

Mitch frowned. "You called to ask me how it's going?"

A pause. Then: "That was just rhetorical. Actually, the question is about the buyers our friend Kostas has lined up. I'm with the cars right now and we're about to head out in a while. I was just wondering if you had any idea when Ted's buyers are due to show up."

"How would I know? Look, *slick*, I gave you Kostas. That's our deal. You want to nail those other guys, you do your own homework. But I'll tell you one thing. You keep nagging Kostas about his buyers and you might as well wear a sign saying you're out to bust him." He took a deep breath. "This your first week on the job or what?" Mitch hung up without another word. Idiot cops.

At ten to twelve, Mitch parked his Volvo three blocks from Al Lucci's house and headed to the old man's place on foot. When he got a couple of doors from it, he saw Alphonse walking slowly toward the front door, studying what appeared to be mail in his hands. Alphonse was wearing dark dress slacks, a white shirt, and a red tie. Mitch watched him go into the house and then took in the neighborhood for a moment. All quiet. Not one person was outside. It was overcast but warm, so Mitch unzipped his leather jacket, patted the nine in the side pocket of his coat, and moved toward the door. Once there, he pressed the doorbell and stood off to the side. When the old man opened the inside door, all he could see through the screen was the back of Mitch's head and jacket.

"What is it?" Alphonse asked, sounding irritated.

At that, Mitch spun quickly and grabbed the screen-door handle. He yanked it and entered the house, pushing the confused Alphonse backward as he did. Inside the foyer, Mitch shut the door behind him and pulled the nine from his pocket. He shoved the barrel into Lucci's face and grabbed the small man by the back of his neck.

"Shut your mouth and listen," Mitch said in a low but clear voice.

"The hell?" was the best Alphonse could come back with at first. He belched in fear and confusion as his mouth dropped open. He recognized the intruder immediately, but it took him a few seconds to put a name to the face. When he did, he asked, "Bosco, right? Why you? Why? Why the hell are you here?"

Mitch tightened his grip on the old man's neck. "Because we're going to go and do some repair work. You and me, right now. If you keep your mouth shut and cooperate, this'll go a whole lot easier. You understand?" He pushed the gun into Al's chin lightly.

Alphonse frowned like he was in great pain. His stomach twitched and he fought, unsuccessfully, to hold back a fart. "What are you talking about here, Bosco?"

Mitch squeezed the neck again and glanced around the living room. He noticed how neat the place was. How old but well preserved the dark furniture looked. "Don't worry," he said as he refocused on Alphonse. "Just do what I say and this'll go fast and smooth. You have your car keys on you?"

Alphonse nodded, still frowning deeply. His mouth was open like it was difficult to breath.

"Good. You have the keys to your place on North Federal?" He paused to recall the name. "The Garlic Bulb Too?"

Again the old man nodded.

"Then we're off." He shot Al a wink.

Mitch walked the Cheese Man through the house and to the garage on the south side of it. When they got to his pale-blue Ford Escort, Mitch ordered Al behind the wheel and he himself eased into the passenger seat. Poor Al was shaking mildly but noticeably by now, and he looked about ready to cry. But he followed Mitch's instructions without a word. He backed carefully out of the garage and closed the door with the remote, then moved down the driveway and out into the street. Alphonse drove to his second pizza joint—on Federal, near Speer Boulevard—in a heavy silence that was broken only occasionally by Mitch's telling the old man to keep his eyes on the road. Alphonse couldn't resist glancing from time to time at the guy next to him with the gun.

When they stopped in front of the restaurant, Mitch instructed the driver to keep going and pull around into the alley in the rear. Al did as he was told and finally parked next to two overflowing Dumpsters immediately behind a metal door with the word "Bulb" stenciled on it.

"You got the keys for the back door, right?" Mitch barked when Al had shut off the engine.

The old man nodded, staring down at the gun in Mitch's hand. "What are you going to do?" he finally asked in a weak voice.

"Let's go inside and I'll tell you."

With that, both men got out of the car and walked the few steps to the rear door. It took Al nearly two minutes to get the right key into the lock and open the door, but Mitch stayed fairly patient. When they had walked inside, Mitch pushed the metal door behind them shut with his left foot. They stood in the narrow kitchen. The lights were out, but a tiny amount of daylight was filtering in unevenly from several windows on the back wall. Mitch squinted as he adjusted to the darkened room. The place smelled like someone had spilled ammonia on a stale pizza.

"Okay, Mr. Lucci," Mitch said when he was done looking around. "Here's the deal. I hate to give you bad news, but you're dead. There's no discussion about that. You won't sell to Disanto, so we figure your daughter will sell to Niles." He paused. "Niles and me."

Alphonse was staring at Mitch's mouth as he spoke, barely comprehending the words coming out of it. "My daughter," he offered feebly.

Mitch nodded. "We know she isn't anywhere near as stubborn as you are about the whole thing. With you gone, she sells to us."

By now Alphonse was getting more centered. "Who's this

us? Freddy Disanto said the development project was done. A wash."

"It is as far as he's concerned. But not as far as the people in Arizona go. It's still in the hopper."

"Then I'll sell to them." Going for a business tone, the old man straightened the glasses on his nose and attempted to do the same thing with his shoulders. "I'm not that stubborn that I can't come to terms with you here, Bosco."

"It's too late for that." Mitch nodded again. "Me just bringing you here like this is kidnapping. No way we're going to work with you. There's no way we *can* work with you anymore. Not after what I just did." He glanced at the nine in his right hand.

"Since when are you part of the Arizona group?"

"Since don't worry about it. You don't need to know about the business end of things."

Alphonse glanced off and considered that. When he looked back at Mitch his eyes narrowed. "So you shoot me right here and now and you don't think that's not going to raise a few questions? Right here in my own kitchen. Sheri might be easier to work with than me, but she's no moron. Neither are the police. If I'm dead, so is any deal you have for my restaurant."

"That's why I'm not going to shoot you, Mr. Lucci," Mitch responded, sounding almost bored now. "You're going to have an accident, and no one will know about me even being here. Then, after a little bit of grieving, your daughter should be pretty open to our offer."

"An accident?" Alphonse sounded less sure of himself again.

"That's the plan. I had dinner here the other night and I studied the layout pretty well. I saw that high balcony you got out there in the main room." He threw his head toward the double doors leading to the restaurant. Moving the nine in that general direction, he motioned for the little man to walk to the other room. "Come on, I'll show you how it works."

Alphonse frowned again but started moving toward the doors. When they got into the dining room, he stopped and looked back at Mitch. The room was slightly better lit than the kitchen, the first floor being about the size of a typical 7-Eleven. A couple dozen tables were arranged throughout. None had tablecloths; their ancient, hard oak tops were exposed.

"There it is," Mitch said as he pointed to the stairs leading to an open second-floor balcony, about fourteen feet higher than the ground floor. The balcony ceiling was another ten feet over that.

"There what is?" Alphonse asked, studying the second floor.

"Your diving board." He looked back down at the Cheese Man. "You must have a ladder around here somewhere. Am I right?"

Alphonse's mouth was wide open now, and he again stared at Mitch. He nodded once. "So?"

"So, you're going to get the ladder out and climb up there to change a light bulb in that chandelier. Only, an old guy like you, you'll probably lose your sense of balance and fall all the way down here." He nodded to the floor. "Accidents like that happen all the time to headstrong old farts like you." Mitch was smiling when he finished.

The little man took a couple of steps toward the middle of the room and looked up at the ornate chandelier hanging partially over the balcony and partially over the main floor. He quickly figured that, if he was on top of a ladder in the balcony and fell, he'd come down a good twenty feet or more. Far enough that he'd never get up and walk away from the spot. He glanced back at Mitch, a quizzical grin spreading across his face.

"You really think I'm going to march up there, up a ladder like that, and just jump?"

"That's about exactly what I think."

"Why the hell would I do that?" He took a step back toward Mitch.

"Because, if you don't, I will shoot you."

"Then fire away, Bosco." Al nodded. "I'd rather go out like that and screw up your plans. That's a no-brainer."

Mitch shrugged, the smile remaining on his face. "It would seem so at first glance, and the end result is the same as far as you're concerned. You're totally dead either way." He paused for a moment. "But it'll be a whole lot easier on that wife of yours if you fall off the ladder."

"Maria?"

"Whatever the old bag's name is. See, if I have to shoot you, I'm going to do the same to her, too. You both die. But if you take the fall, she lives. The choice is yours, really, but I bet if we polled your family on the matter they'd probably say you should climb up the ladder."

33

Freddy the D. was running a few minutes later than he'd hoped that Saturday morning, but there was enough slack time in his plan that he wasn't much worried. Kostas wasn't expecting him until noon, and he'd still beat that by a bit. He left his house at eleven-fifteen, which got him just down the street from Kostas's scrap yard at a quarter to twelve. He'd meant to be there by eleven-thirty, but he still had time. The D. eased his new Infiniti to the curb, just around the corner from Ted's place, and carefully locked his door. He buttoned his overcoat and put on his sunglasses, although, given that it was warm and cloudy, he really didn't need either of them. Still, the D. hardly wanted to be easily recognizable.

Walking up the alley to Ted's back door, the D. flashed on the two people he hated most in the whole world: Alphonse Lucci and Niles Macmillan. In no particular order. Lucci for being stubborn and Niles for being such a pushy little pecker. The D. was glad he was rid of both of them, although, as long as he'd been in the killing business recently, he wondered if he shouldn't have just wasted old man Lucci weeks ago. Made short work of everything. Made it a go for the development of the West Side block. Screw it, he reasoned as he got near Ted's office. That project could still flop even if they did buy Lucci's place. Not to mention, who wants to have Niles Macmillan around twenty-four hours a day? Certainly not Freddy Disanto. Let Mitch Bosco worry about that mother, if indeed Mitch was in with the Arizona boys now. As for the Cheese Man, the D. might just make it a point to give him a headache or two sometime down the road. Just on principle, for all the grief that the old man had caused him lately.

The D. shook his head in mild disgust as he reached for Ted's back-door handle. He'd think more about Alphonse Lucci later. Now it was show time, and the D. wanted to move as quickly as possible. As he twisted the handle, he smacked the door with the flat of his left hand to let the man inside know he was there.

Ted Kostas had barely slept the night before. He'd jumped up about every half-hour to check the vintage brown suitcase sitting at the foot of his bed. Then he'd contemplated the score he was about to make that Saturday, smoking a cigarette to calm himself down before heading back to bed. When the long night finally ended, he was starving. He went to his scrap yard shortly before ten o'clock, bringing along the suitcase and his handsome wood-handled Smith & Wesson .38 Special. He stopped on the way in and picked up four Egg McMuffins, four orders of hash browns, and three coffees to get him going. Sitting at his desk, the suitcase touching his leg and the .38 resting next to the food on his desk, Ted felt pretty good after a while. He didn't smell so good, given that he hadn't showered that morning.

Or the morning before, either, come to think of it. But there would be plenty of time for personal hygiene when he was done moving the Jags.

As he ate, Ted Kostas thought of Freddy Disanto. Could there be a way to keep some of his thirty thousand in cash from the crazy Italian? True, the D. would be saving his life. A very important item if Ted was going to sell the cars for a profit and be around to enjoy it. But giving up *all* the cash didn't have nearly as much appeal that morning as it had had when the D. first brought up the topic the day before. Ted sat nursing his coffee and smoking at the desk for a long time after he'd finished eating. Must have run the problem over in his mind a hundred times before he heard the hand slap on his door and turned to see Freddy Disanto walk into his office. By then, the best that Ted Kostas had come up with was that he'd negotiate with the D. Let him know that all the cash in the suitcase was simply too much to pay. Tell him that the highest he'd go was twenty-five thousand. Cash money, take it or leave it. He had even pulled five thousand from the old suitcase and stuck it in his middle desk drawer. Hell, Kostas thought, if the D. just took the cash and left, he could handle that asshole Todd guy and his brother all by himself. After all, Ted was the one with the .38.

"Having a little lunch there, are we?" the D. asked casually as he walked into the room. He tucked his sunglasses into his coat pocket and glanced around. It was a tiny space, and he had to squint at first, because there was only one small desk lamp on and very little light was filtering in through the two filthy back windows. A small, square purple satin pillow with the words "Las Vegas" embroidered on it caught his eye. He smiled and picked the pillow up from where it was sitting on a shelf next to a row of sagging auto-parts books.

"Very nice meal there, Ted," he continued as he turned

toward Kostas. He nodded at the food wrappers on the desk. "You just come off a month-long fast or something?"

Ted frowned for a second, glanced back at the wrappers and then up at the D. again. "Huh?"

Freddy rolled his eyes almost imperceptibly. "Forget it. You bring everything? I see the .38 there. How about the money?"

"I thought you said you'd be here at noon." His forehead creased in concern. "Why you so early?"

"I wanted to spend more time with you, seeing as how we had so much fun yesterday." The D. moved the two steps across the room to put him next to his host. "What difference does it make, me being a few minutes early? The point is, we got work to do."

Holding the pillow in his left hand, the D. bent over and reached across the desktop to grab the .38. With one hand, he spun the chamber to make sure it was loaded. He also saw that it wasn't locked. Then he looked back down at Ted.

"So far, so good," the D. said. "Where's the money? Give me a look at it before I get into position."

Ted took a sip from coffee that by now was as cold as wet concrete. Time to negotiate. He took a deep breath and nodded once toward the brown bag at his side on the floor. Bending over to that side, he snapped open the two latches on the case. Then he lifted the leather bag and tipped the thing slightly toward the D., exposing lots of green cash.

"It's right here in the case." Ted shut the suitcase again and straightened up. "But I think we have to talk about something first." He squinted slightly, pausing to check for a reaction from the D., who seemed to be standing practically on top of him by now.

What Freddy Disanto did at that point was definitely a reaction, but nothing that Ted Kostas had anticipated as he ate breakfast. Certainly it wasn't anything like what he had hoped for. With the hint of a smile on his face, the D. moved his left hand deftly and pulled the purple pillow down on top of Kostas's head. Then, just as smoothly, he brought up his other hand and jammed the barrel of the .38 down onto it, hard. Without a word, the D. fired the Smith & Wesson pistol once. It made a loud pop, but the pillow helped muffle the sound, as Disanto had hoped. The room smelled like burnt metal as the man at the desk jerked tightly and then slumped back and down in his chair.

Freddy Disanto tossed the pillow off to the side and glanced around the room again. On a bench next to the desk, he spotted a couple of dirty work rags. He picked up one and carefully wiped down Ted's .38. That finished, he set the gun on the desktop, bent over, and hoisted the brown suitcase. It felt like what he imagined thirty thousand dollars weighed. The D. grinned quickly and looked back down at Ted Kostas.

"I told you this thing'd be all over before you knew it," the D. said softly. Within seconds, he was back outside in the alley, wiping down the door handle on both sides with the work rag. That done, he walked quietly to his car. The sky seemed to be clearing up a little, he thought as he put his shades back on.

Todd Janek was loose but excited as he pulled the dark-blue Jaguar into the parking lot at precisely twelve-thirty. Detective Carl Morris followed close behind in a green version of the same vehicle. When they both shut off their engines and got out of their respective cars, Detective Morris walked over to Todd and handed him the car keys. Todd merely nodded, and the detective turned and walked toward the front gate, as Ted Kostas had instructed. Putting Morris's keys with his own, Todd dropped them into a large manila envelope he was carrying. He then made a quick survey of the scrap yard, noticing that the two aging Dobermans were acting strange. Presumably, they would be out of their pen. And from what Janek had seen the day before, neither of them was what one would call particularly ambitious. But here they were, both just sort of slouched against the front door, barely acknowledging the strangers who'd just arrived.

Then Todd noticed something that made his stomach drop. It was in the dog pen. Or, rather, not in the pen. Kostas had said he'd leave a suitcase full of money in with the dogs. Todd frowned and looked at the front window to the office. He half expected to see the old Greek looking out to make sure the transaction went as planned. But no one was in sight. Then he walked cautiously to the office door. Neither of the dogs responded much; one just sort of moaned softly. Instinctively, Todd's free hand, his right, moved toward the small of his back, where he kept his service revolver. Again he glanced at the dog pen. He couldn't see the suitcase from that angle, either.

Standing directly in front of the door, Todd took a long moment to figure his options. He really had only one. Leaning forward, he dropped the envelope and pounded three times on the door with the meat of his left fist. He waited for what seemed to be minutes, and then he pounded again. Louder and longer this time. Again nothing, so he reached back farther and pulled out the Ed Brown Classic Custom .45 he carried. Even in a tense moment like this, Janek marveled at how sleek the chrome, steel, and wood looked. He loved his piece. Then he pounded on the door four more times, loudly, while calling out "Kostas!" repeatedly.

No response, so he grabbed the door handle and turned it. He was half surprised that it was unlocked. Taking a deep breath, he pushed the door open. Both dogs bolted inside as he did. Todd squinted into the unlit outer-office area. Through the open door to the small room in the rear, he could see the back of Ted Kostas's head. Or, rather, what used to be his head. The bloody remains were resting quietly on the top of the swivel chair. Todd felt his stomach tighten, and he thought he might get sick. Suddenly, one of the dogs moved back and began to nuzzle the area around Ted Kostas's neck. The bloody head rolled to its right a shade and then dropped out of sight below the chair top. Todd held his automatic up high while he reached inside his windbreaker for the small cell phone he kept there. When he finished calling his backup, he waited for them quietly, and did not go into Ted's office alone.

"No kidding this changes things, Karen." Todd was again speaking into his cell phone. By now he and the three police detectives had secured the murder scene, and he was standing in the middle of Ted's tiny office. His eyes kept wandering to the desktop and all the McDonald's wrappers and empty coffee cups. Hell of a last meal. "I mean, we got Kostas, but not the way we planned."

"What else do you have?" Karen asked from her end.

"Well, we got a murder weapon that looks all smudged up with grease or something. Good luck getting any decent prints off of it." Todd glanced around again. "We got a bloody pillow that looks like it's been fired through. Probably used to quiet the shot. We got no forced entry, no suitcase with money, no eyewitnesses—not yet, anyway—and, last but not least, we got no Jaguar sting. In other words, we got shit."

"Not nearly as much as Mr. Kostas," Karen came back. "Keep that in mind." She thought for a moment. "Do you think Mitch Bosco had anything to do with this? He knew the money would be there."

"Unlikely." Todd took a deep breath. "For one thing, I

talked to him a little while ago and he was still at home. This body looks pretty fresh. I don't think the timing is right for Bosco to get down here, kill Kostas, and get home to take my call. And for another thing, I doubt that Bosco would be dumb enough to try a stunt like this, knowing we'd being thinking of him first."

"That may be, but let's round him up anyhow." Karen was pacing her kitchen as she spoke. "I'll send a car over to grab him. If we're screwed on this deal, then so is he. No plea bargain on Monday." She stopped and thought for a long time. "You-know-what's going to hit the fan with the DA over this thing, and I don't want to even think about the press we're going to get. I want to have someone waiting to catch the flak. Someone besides us, that is. It may as well be Mitch Bosco."

Todd considered that. "What do you mean, we? This was your baby, Karen. You were the one who made all the decisions on Bosco and Kostas. They were your guys."

Karen glanced at the phone in her hand. "You know what I really like about you, Todd? It's your loyalty. Here you are, antsy to play hero when all you have to do is pop one elderly fence. Then things go south and you're running for cover before I can even get down there to view the body."

"All I'm saying is, you were the one who dug up Bosco and you were the one who lined this thing up. That's all I'm saying."

"I know exactly what you're saying, Todd. Try not to mess up the crime scene, okay? Just do me that one little favor. And start talking to the neighbors. See if anyone saw anything. I'll be there in twenty minutes."

When she hung up, Karen Maples stood silently in her kitchen for several minutes, half wishing she'd taken her parents' advice and gone into contract law.

34

By the time Streeter pulled up in front of the Garlic Bulb Too, he had just about given up on finding Alphonse Lucci. The Garlic Bulb itself had been closed and empty when he went there. He'd even walked around the whole building, but, clearly, no one was inside. Then, on the drive over to the second restaurant, his lack of sleep started catching up with him. He figured, if the Cheese Man wasn't here at the Bulb Too, he'd skip going to his catering office and just head back to the church. Maybe catch a nap and hope that Alphonse would get one of the messages and show up on his own. Walking to the front door of the second Bulb and seeing that the place wouldn't be open until five-thirty didn't do much to lift his spirits.

He stood on the sidewalk for a moment, glancing at the sky. The sun was starting to poke through the clouds, but Streeter was by now as sleepy as if it were midnight. He took a couple more steps toward the restaurant and idly jiggled the front door. Locked. Then he held one hand up to shield his eyes from the sun and leaned into the window on the door, squinting inside. At first, he saw no signs of life in the large main room. But as he squinted harder, he spotted two figures walking up a long stairway to his right. The one farther up the stairs was clearly Alphonse; he couldn't quite make out the second man. Then both figures stopped and the old man turned and looked down at the guy behind him. They appeared to be arguing. Suddenly, the second man gave Alphonse a push with both hands. When he turned slightly, Streeter recognized him as Mitch Bosco. Mitch was holding something shiny in his right hand and pointing it at the man in front of him. It was a gun.

"Let's get along there, Mr. Lucci," Mitch said, looking up and shaking his head. "No point in dragging this out."

"I've got plenty of cash in my office," Al responded. "Whatever those guys are paying you, I'll top it. Easy."

Mitch shook his head again. "Time to negotiate is long-gone, Mr. Lucci. Now it's time to close the deal. You know I can't let you walk away from this."

Alphonse glanced off, thinking about that. Then he looked back at Mitch. "I'll double it. No kidding. I'll double whatever they're paying."

"I'm afraid not." Mitch reached up with both hands and pushed softly at the little man's chest. "Let's get that ladder and do her." Then he lifted his nine slightly. "Upward we go."

Alphonse turned sluggishly and walked up the remaining stairs. When they got to the top, he moved quietly to a small door off to his right and opened it. Inside was a stepladder that, when folded, was about a foot taller than the old man. He reached in and started to pull it out. Then he stopped and turned to face Mitch.

"Think you can give me a hand here, Bosco?" he asked. "It's the least you can do."

"Just bring it out. It's not like you have to save your strength for anything."

Alphonse faced the ladder again, his mouth opening wide as he sucked for air. He wrestled the ladder out of the closet and dragged it slowly across the carpeting to the rail on the outside of the balcony. Then he stopped, breathing really hard by now and wiping at a crease of sweat over his eyes.

Streeter trotted quickly back to the Buick. Under the driver's seat was his .357. He took the gun out and checked to make sure it was loaded. Back at the front door of the restaurant, he strained to look inside. He could see that Mitch and Alphonse were right next to the balcony edge by now. The old man was opening a small stepladder, while Mitch watched him closely. Streeter debated whether to smash the window on the door and try to get in that way. But he didn't know how the lock worked, and he was afraid that the sudden noise and movement would set Bosco off and start him shooting. Glancing to the side, he figured it would be better to run around to the back of the place. Mitch and Al had probably come in a rear door; maybe it was still unlocked. He broke into a full sprint and ran to the north side of the building, leading to the alley behind it.

"Now I'm supposed to just hop up there and jump off?" Al was saying as he looked at the ladder. It was open and shoved directly against the ornate wrought-iron railing along the balcony.

"You don't have to hop," Mitch responded. "Just climbing will do fine. And I can push you, if that would make it any easier."

Alphonse continued to study the ladder, not moving.

Finally, Mitch tapped his shoulder with the gun. "Like I said, there's no point in dragging this out. You might as well just do it. That is, unless you'd like Maria to get hurt, too."

"There's gotta be a way we can work this thing out," Alphonse said, turning back to Mitch.

"That's exactly what we're doing here. Working it out." He nodded toward the ladder. "So let's get going."

Streeter grabbed the handle on the back door and opened it quickly but carefully, to avoid making noise. He stepped into the kitchen and spotted the double doors leading to the restaurant itself. Glancing from side to side, he moved through the long room and stopped at the doors. Then he pushed one open slowly, straining to spot the balcony. He could hear Alphonse and Mitch Bosco talking off to his left and above him. When he got the door open far enough, he stepped into the main room and looked in that direction. The old man was stepping onto a lower rung of the ladder. Alphonse appeared to be holding the sides of the ladder tightly, moving about as slowly as Streeter had ever seen anyone move. He'd look up toward the top of the ladder and the huge chandelier from time to time, and then back down at Bosco.

"That's right, Mr. Lucci," Mitch was saying. "One step at a time until you get to the top."

"This is crazy, Bosco." Alphonse was sweating freely by now, and his face was completely white. The sweat dripped into his eyes; he pulled one hand off the ladder and wiped at them.

"Tell me about it," Mitch responded. "But just crazy enough to work."

Walking silently toward the stairs, Streeter grabbed his gun with both hands. By the time he made it to the bottom step, the old man had gone up another rung. Streeter couldn't figure out what the two men were doing up there, but it was plain to see that Alphonse was terrified. Looking down at the carpeted steps in front of him, the bounty hunter took them fast and quiet, two at a time until he got near the top. When he stopped there, he could see all of the Cheese Man, who by now had made it halfway up the ladder. Mitch Bosco was standing off to the side with a small automatic pointed at Alphonse's body. Streeter took another step and then raised his .357 toward Mitch.

"Let's hold it right where you are, Bosco," he yelled. "Al, climb down slowly."

Both men on the balcony turned to see where the voice was coming from. Instinctively, Mitch took a step away from it and toward the far side of the ladder, his gun still pointed at Alphonse.

"Streeter?" the old man asked hoarsely. "That you, Streeter?"

"It's me, Al." Streeter took another step up, so he was about ten feet from the ladder. He stared at Mitch. "Drop the gun, Bosco."

Mitch moved behind the ladder till it was partially shielding him from Streeter. He frowned, his eyes darting from the man on the ladder to the man on the stairs. But he said nothing.

"Drop the gun and move away from there," Streeter yelled. "Now!"

"How'd you get here?" Mitch asked, moving even closer to the ladder for protection.

"Never mind." Streeter paused. "What's going on?"

"This guy wants me to climb up here and jump off," Alphonse said, looking down at Mitch. "You believe that? Thinks that'll make it look like I fell by accident. Said he'd shoot both me and Maria if I don't." He took a slow step back down the ladder.

"Get back up there." Mitch's voice was a little hoarse.

Streeter raised his gun to where it was pointed at Bosco's head. "Give it up and put down the gun. The party's over, Bosco. You've got a witness, which means you're finished."

By now, Mitch had worked himself completely behind the ladder. His nine was jammed through it and into Alphonse's side as he stood twisted on the middle rung. Silently, Bosco considered his next move. The old man was above him, wiping at his eyes and moving his head from Mitch to Streeter. Mitch decided he had all of one way out.

"I'm taking Lucci here and we're leaving," he finally said. "Get back down the stairs and out of here. That way I don't have to shoot the old man." He jammed his nine into Alphonse's side.

"Where do you think you're going?" Streeter asked. "There's nowhere to run, Bosco. Give it up before someone gets hurt."

"Can't you just shoot him, Streeter?" Alphonse said. There were three rungs between his feet and the ground. He turned out toward the stairs and away from Mitch, his small left foot lowering itself to the next rung down.

Mitch saw the movement and jammed his gun harder into Alphonse. The old man lost his balance and slid down the remaining rungs, his feet splayed out in front of him and his backside knocking against the steps. It took him all of about a second to hit the ground, landing solidly on his butt. The unexpected motion stunned Mitch for a moment and left him exposed to Streeter, his gun arm dangling through the middle rung of the ladder. The bounty hunter sprang to the top of the stairs and stopped in a half-crouch, his hands holding the .357 extended straight out in front of him. The old man let out a loud groan and rolled onto his side and into a ball on the floor. Mitch tried to get his nine pointed at Streeter, but the ladder prevented that. He fired two shots anyhow; both flew harmlessly a few feet to Streeter's left. Then Mitch pulled his arm back and out of the ladder. As he did, the bounty hunter fired a warning shot over his head, which Mitch ignored. Instead of stopping, he kept bringing his arm back. When it was free of the ladder, he began to turn it on Alphonse. One way or another, he figured, the old man was going to die.

Seeing that, Streeter lowered his .357 and fired another round. It hit Mitch on the outer side of his left shoulder, solidly enough to spin him completely around and land him on the ground, facedown. He made one more attempt to move his gun hand back in the Cheese Man's direction, but instead he went into shock and blacked out.

"Godawmighty," Alphonse yelled out as he struggled to his knees. "This is like *The Untouchables* or something." He stared down at Mitch's back, then got to his feet and turned toward Streeter, who had moved alongside of him. "Nice shot there, Streeter."

The bounty hunter nodded, went to Mitch's side, and kicked the nine away from his hand. That done, he looked over at Alphonse.

"Are you all right, Al?"

The little man nodded, his mouth still open wide. "If I don't have a heart attack here, I think I'll make it." He paused. "Is Bosco dead?"

Streeter shook his head. "But you better call 911 fast. He doesn't look all that good."

"He never did," Alphonse said as he straightened his glasses. "Let him sit there for a while. That schmuck had his way, I'd be splattered all over the floor by now." Then he looked up hard at Streeter. "How'd you know to come over here just now?"

Streeter shrugged. "I was doing a little digging around

this morning and I wanted to talk to you about what I found."

"Digging into my restaurant deal?"

"Yeah."

"Why? I told you the other day that all this business was finished."

"I guess you did, but it didn't make any sense, ending all of a sudden like that."

Alphonse shook his head. "You're a bigger worrier than me, and that's going some." He stared down at Mitch again. "Which right about now is something I'm pretty happy about."

"I doubt if he feels the same as you on that one." Streeter knelt down and checked Mitch's pulse. Then he glanced up at Alphonse. "You better make that call right now. This guy's starting to fade on us."

35

They were deep into their third bottle of Al's dago-red house wine. It tasted like ketchup run amok but had enough attitude to get them feeling friendly and comfortably disoriented. Little Al was standing next to the best table in the Garlic Bulb, holding a glass of the stuff at shoulder level. He was wearing his standard-issue dark suit and red tie, white shirt buttoned to the top. But the smile smeared across his face let them know he was in an unusual mood.

"To Streeter," the Cheese Man said. "Guy that saved the family and made things right again." He glanced over at the bounty hunter, who was sitting between Frank and Ronnie. "To your whole gang there, Streeter. Thanks for getting me outa the woods like that."

Streeter nodded, and all four of them clinked glasses.

"I mean it," Al continued when they'd finished the toast. "I owe you plenty. If you woulda dropped the whole thing like I asked"—he shook his head—"I'd be history by now."

"What ever happened to the big bad hit man?" Frank asked.

"Detective Carey tells me he's going to make it, all right," Streeter replied. "But apparently he's none too thrilled with the prospect. He's facing more charges than I can remember off the top of my head. I hear he's scrambling to make a deal with the DA, who isn't interested in making any more deals with him. Not after that Ted Kostas fiasco."

"Can you blame him after what happened at that junk-yard last week?" Frank said. In his expensive dark-brown suit and club tie, he looked like a banker. He studied the cigar burning in his right hand and then looked over at the dirty dishes on the table. "They go out there to take Kostas off for those hot cars and he ends up getting splattered all over his own office with his own gun."

"The DA's people came off looking like total jerks in the media," Ronnie said. She took another sip from her wine-glass. "Especially on TV. It sounds like the deputy who set up that sting up is going to be doing traffic court and dog-barking complaints for the next few years."

Streeter glanced at her. She was wearing a white cotton blouse and a simple navy skirt. Easy on the makeup and easy on the eye. Nothing like how she looked the night she scammed Ted Kostas. "How do you feel about your date from that one night getting killed the way he did?" he asked her.

"It's not like we were going together or anything, but I felt sorry for old Teddy," she said. "He was about as pathetic as they come, but he sure didn't deserve what he got."

"I hate to bad-mouth the dead, but I agree with your appraisal, Ronnie," Frank interjected. "It doesn't sound like he'll be missed all that much by anyone." He paused. "I'm not surprised about that deputy getting demoted, though. It doesn't look so good when your people run into a place to arrest someone and they find him all dead like that and you don't have any idea who did the thing. Not a clue."

"You got that right," Streeter said, nodding. "At any rate, Mitch is trying to make a deal with the local guys for his testimony against the people down in Arizona who set him up to kill Al. He wants to get a few hundred years knocked off his potential sentence so he has a shot at getting out of prison in this lifetime. Carey says that the DA seems mildly interested, but it's the feds who are really putting the pressure on him to talk."

"Don't hold your breath on that one," Frank said. He studied his partner. "Who do you think it was that actually killed Mr. Kostas, Street?"

Streeter shook his head. "I wouldn't know. Maybe I've got an educated guess, but I've got nothing to back it up with. The best I can figure out is that he made arrangements with someone to help him with the deal and that someone turned on him. Probably to get the money, although Carey tells me they found five thousand in cash in the office. Evidently the police were expecting about thirty thousand on hand." He shrugged. "Either that or one of the buyers showed up early and it got out of hand for some reason."

"Who's your educated guess?" Ronnie asked.

"I have to admit that the name Freddy Disanto has crossed my mind, but that's probably way off the mark. The only reason I say that is because of his connection to Mitch Bosco. One thing for sure—whoever it was, they're home free now."

Al worked into that one. "If you're right about Freddy, it really corks me royally that he'll never have to answer for it. Just like with him killing that guy up in Wyoming. The D. is one of those rare guys that can get away with murder and even make a few bucks off of it. Ain't no one I ever heard of tough enough to go after the D. Or crazy enough, for that matter."

"He can't go on like that forever," the bounty hunter said.

Al nodded, set his wine down, and put both hands on the table, leaning in slightly. His glasses looked huge against his white skin and small eyes, which seemed to be tearing up. "I gotta say, this situation was one major pain in the ass, but I think me and my family's all the better for it.

"Take Sheri. She tells me now she wants to spend a lot more time with Nicky when he gets home in a couple of weeks. Kid's doing great in rehab, and he says he wants to come work in the restaurant business. Course, he still has that car theft to deal with." Al nodded slowly, like he was spreading great insights. "But he will have quite a good chance to learn the business pretty soon. I'm retiring, and Sheri's taking over. I'm gonna do some traveling with Maria. We been talking about it the last few days. Back to Italy, like we always planned on but never got around to actually doing. Neither of us is getting any younger and I figure it's time I stop trying to act like James Cagney all over the place and enjoy Maria a lot more."

"No more card games?" Streeter asked.

"You got that one right." The old man's face turned suddenly stern. "Who the hell needs to deal with the likes of Freddy the D. and all those crazy punks running around shooting up my walls? I tell you, no more of that stuff for me. Time for me to appreciate what I got and knock off the gangster stuff."

36

Freddy the D. was feeling so good when he left his girlfriend's house that night that he even gave a passing thought to maybe having sex with his wife. That weekend might work. Definitely not when he got home later. It was just before twelve, and he'd been with Candy since right after his regular Thursday lunch at Pagliacci's. Ten hours of pure sex and a ton of wine. I still got it, even at my age, he thought. Of course, who wouldn't have the energy and stamina with Candy? Man oh man, she had a build on her. That woman could give a corpse a wet dream. Plus, she wouldn't be pushing forty for another twenty years, give or take. By then, the D. knew, he'd have replaced her at least three or four times. Yes indeed, life was truly good. Plenty of poontang, food, and wine. What else do you need? the D. asked himself. Even if that big development deal with the Arizona people fell through, Disanto had managed to come away with twenty-five grand and his skin. Which is more than Mitch

Bosco and old Niles and company could say right about now. Bosco was getting the FBI very interested in Niles and his people, which meant that everyone involved would probably be doing some serious time over the failed project. Everyone, that is, except for Freddy "the D." Disanto.

As he walked to his car, he flashed on his wife again. It had been so long since they'd really touched that he had to struggle to recall what Angie was like in the sack. He used to be so incredibly hot for her, too. Those first couple of years they were married, hell, he nearly killed himself in the bedroom with her. But then came four kids, more than a few extra pounds, and the hint of a mustache. Not to mention her attitude. Angie would come at him sometimes lately like a constipated wolf. All those accusations. "Where you been?" "Why do you smell like that?" Forget about it. Most of the time, he felt like smacking her around the room. More often than not, he would.

What can I do? he wondered. Changes in old Angie's body, and the feelings for her changed, too. Freddy didn't understand all that, but he didn't fight it, either. That's how men act in these circumstances. At least Angie was a good mother, and she could still cook better than a pro when she got in the right mind-set.

At first he didn't see the man leaning against his Infiniti. There were no streetlights near where he parked in the alley off 43rd Street. But then the guy coughed lightly and Freddy spotted him. The D. squinted in the moonlight. He was in too good a mood right then to get very pissed off. When he came within about twenty feet of his car, he just waved a hand.

"Move it along, pal," he said in a tired voice. "It's too late at night for games."

"You got a nice ride here, man." The voice was casual and the form moved a bit, though in no obvious hurry.

Freddy took a few more steps and he could see that it was a man about his height but with a much slimmer build. Even in the bad light, there was something familiar about the face. The voice and accent, too.

"Like that's any of your fucking business." This time the D. put some muscle in his tone. Last thing he wanted now was to have to take the time to kick the shit out of some Mexican. He was becoming vaguely aware of a growing Chianti headache.

"Forget your car, man. You're my business, Fredo."

He definitely knew that voice. By now the D. was only ten feet from his car.

"Get off the car or you're gonna be one fucked-up unit," the D. growled. Suddenly, it came to Freddy. This had to be him. "You!" he yelled. The D. stopped walking and began to reach down to his ankle holster. As he did he was aware of a motion behind him and the whooshing sound of something large moving through the air. An instant later he felt a jolt of hot pain from the top right side of his head shooting all the way down that side of his body and leg to his foot. It was like one long nerve on fire.

The D. dropped to both knees so fast he couldn't get his hands out to help break the fall. Once his knees hit the ground he tried to reach out. But he kept going and ended up with his face in the dirt and gravel. His butt was up in the air and his hands were flung lamely out to either side. Seeing his breath burst out around his face, he realized how cold the autumn night air really was. He stayed in that position for a moment and then got his left hand up under his chest. The D. managed to push himself up to nearly a kneeling position, but he knew that he had little control over his right side. His head felt like it was in flames, and when he tried to say something, the best he could do was make a hoarse gurgling sound.

The man leaning against the car stepped toward him and bent over. "No, man. You got it all wrong. You the fucked-up unit here."

Freddy could see the man was smiling, so he reached out with his left hand to grab at his face. Another whooshing sound, this time slower. Another jolt to the top of his head. Not nearly as hard, but still mean. This time, the D.'s face practically flew back down to the ground. He could feel the side of one cheek scrape against the stones, and he had no energy or motor control to move. Then he thought he heard a clunking sound, like something hollow being thrown on the ground next to him. A second or so later he could feel a hand grabbing the hair on the top of his head from behind and pulling it back. He wanted to fight, but there was no way his body would respond as he lay there on the gravel with only his head lifted. It forced him to look at the man in front of him. The other guy, the one who by now was on top of him holding up his head, Freddy could not see.

"You're not so tough now, are you?" the man in front of him asked. "Dago piece of shit. You know what this is all about, don't you?"

The D. knew, but the best he could do was spit weakly in the man's direction.

"Still got a little fight, huh?" The man smiled. He nodded to the guy kneeling on Freddy Disanto. "End it now."

The man behind let go of the hair, and Freddy's face fell back to the ground. Then he pulled a two-foot piece of piano wire from his back pocket, wrapping an end around each of his hands. He tugged it quickly one time. The guy in front of the D. lifted his head again while the other man worked the wire under his chin and around his neck. With both of his hands crossed over behind Freddy's neck, he suddenly pulled hard with each. Freddy's windpipe broke right away under the intense pressure from the wire, but it was still another minute or so before he stopped breathing entirely.

"How you like that, tough-guy wop? Don't feel so good, huh?" The man from in front asked, glaring down at the D.'s body.

The two men then turned him over and checked for any signs of life. There were none. They emptied Freddy's pockets of everything. When they stood up, the quiet one grabbed the aluminum bat he'd used, wiped his fingerprints from it with his red handkerchief, and tossed it into the bushes in front of the Infiniti. Without a word, they walked quickly from the alley and two blocks to the west, where their pickup was parked. Once inside, the driver turned to the man who had garroted Freddy Disanto.

"That's about the same chance he gave Albert, huh?" Manny Ramirez asked the passenger.

Neal Ringo nodded in the darkness. "Let's get a move on. It's a long way back down to New Orleans."

"You got that about right," Manny said as he turned on the engine. "A long way. Ain't no one gonna figure out it was us did this, but I got a feeling we'll be down there for a while." He shoved the gear shift into first and pulled away from the curb. After about a block he glanced over at Neal for a second. "You know, man, it's like the old days. The Ramirez Boys ride again. That dumb Albert might have been useless as shit dust half the time, but he was one of us. Feels good, what we just did, huh?"

Neal grunted in agreement, but he was starting to see a pattern emerging. Albert Hepp and now Freddy Disanto. Manny's time would come, too. So would his. Neal closed his eyes and slumped down in his seat. Might as well sleep for as much of the ride as he could.